BLOOD

MOON

A RILEY HUNTER NOVEL

AMANDA LYNN

∞ ∞ ∞

Cover designed by Coverinked Book Cover Design
http://coverinked.com/

This book is a work of fiction. Names, characters, places, and incidents either are products of the author's imagination or are used fictitiously. Any resemblance to actual persons, living or dead, events, or locales is entirely coincidental.

Amanda Lynn
Visit my website at https://amandalynnauthor.com/

Printed in the United States of America

First Printing: May 2019
Amanda Lynn

ISBN-9781093145090

CONTENTS

FOR MY HUSBAND, THANK YOU
FOR YOUR UNWAVERING SUPPORT.
AND FOR TAKING CARE OF
EVERYTHING DURING THOSE
LONG NIGHTS OF WRITING AND
EDITING.

"Twenty years from now you will be more disappointed by the things that you didn't do than by the ones you did do."
-Mark Twain

CHAPTER 1

I t felt good to sit at my desk again. Even though I wouldn't be officially re-opening the office to new business for another week, just being there and getting everything ready for my clients was relaxing. It had been almost two-and-a-half months since Malus kidnapped me with the intention of turning me into a vampire and forcing me to become one of his followers, and things were finally getting back to normal—well, as normal as they could anyway.

Lucian had rallied several vampires and werewolves to come to my rescue during my abduction, but somehow, Malus managed to escape. We hadn't seen or heard from him since that night, but we knew it was only a matter of time before he remerged; he was too obsessed with his plan to announce the existence of vampires to the world. Eventually, he'd resurface. Whether it was in Louisville, or somewhere else, was yet to be seen.

We also still weren't sure if Jessica, the missing person I'd been trying to find—who'd been turned into a vampire and stabbed me during the chaos of the fight between Malus' followers and my rescue team—fled with him or not. Before their scents faded and could no longer be tracked, they were still traveling in opposite directions. But that didn't mean they couldn't have met up later at a pre-determined rendezvous point.

I'd tried to hate Jessica for attempting to kill me, especially since she would've succeeded if it hadn't been for Lucian, but I couldn't. She was only trying to get revenge for her lover, who I'd killed. But it technically wasn't my fault since he attacked me and would've slaughtered me if I hadn't killed him first. I'd never taken someone's life before, and it was purely out of self-defense, but she obviously didn't see it that way. And I had to admit that most of the time I didn't either. At the end of the day, his death was still on my hands, and I didn't blame her for wanting someone to pay for it.

Luckily, Lucian was able to get to me before I bled out in the middle of the field. He gave me a choice; and fearing death and never seeing my family or Lucian again, I chose to become a vampire.

I couldn't have asked for a better teacher and mentor than Lucian. Being a vampire was so different from being a human, and at times, it had been really hard to get used to the changes. But Lucian was there every step of the way to give advice and guidance through the process.

The biggest obstacle, for me, was the constant craving of blood. The metamorphosis that a human body went through during and right after the Becoming required much more blood to be consumed in comparison to someone who'd already been a vampire for a while. I was put on a set schedule of a full glass of the red stuff every two hours. And those first couple of weeks were excruciating. I felt like I was constantly starving and would count down the minutes until I could get my hands on more blood. There were moments when I really thought I was going to lose it. Lucian assured me it was normal to crave blood like that during the initial adjustment period, and when my body didn't need as much anymore, the cravings would calm down.

Thankfully, he was right. I was still attracted to blood, like all vampires, but I was finally over the initial bloodlust, and I wasn't constantly thinking about getting my hands, or teeth, on another blood bag every second of the day. I could also now refrain from what I called, *vamping out,* and was able to keep my eyes from changing and my teeth retracted when I was around blood or humans—most of the time.

We were predators by nature, and when we were near our food source, we went into predator mode; our teeth elongated for the bite, and our eyes illuminated iridescently, allowing for better night vision and to see everything more clearly in general. It allowed us to see every small movement of what we tracked, whether it was an opponent or prey. And I'm not going to lie, it was both scary and exciting all at the same time.

The next biggest obstacle was controlling my emotions. Ever since I'd become a vampire, they tended to run a little on the extreme side, and I had almost no control over them. I'd fast learned that with heightened senses, also came the burden of heightened emotions. Things that should've barely registered on my '*things that piss me off meter*', were suddenly topping the charts. I had mood swings that would rival any pregnant woman, and since I couldn't control them, it only served to piss me off even more. And if I didn't get them under control fast enough, a pulsing numbness would begin to throb in my chest.

Lucian confirmed the volatile emotions were normal—the weird pulsing sensation . . . not so much. I just couldn't catch a break. First, I was an abnormal human who could sense vampires. Now, I was an abnormal vampire whose chest began humming every time I got mad. What the fuck was wrong with me?

That vampire sensing ability—the catalyst for the entire chain of events that led to my current non-human status had only intensified since I'd become a vampire. I could now sense another vampire from almost double the distance as before. And sometimes, I swear I could even distinguish who it was.

As much as I liked being with Lucian and staying with him in his basement apartment under the club, *Silver Moon*, I'd started to become homesick and desperately wanted to return to some kind of normalcy in my life, so I moved back into my apartment last week. I was too used to being independent, and just because I was head-over-heels for Lucian, didn't mean I was ready to throw my life away and follow him around like a lost puppy. This thing between us was still so new, and I didn't want to rush the relationship.

Because let's face it, it would be so easy to do. The pull toward him had only strengthened since he turned me, and deep down, I had this primal desire that only wanted Lucian— everything else be damned. And I was only holding that yearning back with sheer willpower and stubbornness. I'd been single for most of my adult life before Lucian came into the picture, and I wanted to take it slow and let things progress naturally of their own accord—not because of some magnetic attraction that I still wasn't completely convinced wasn't supernatural in origin. If the day ever did come when we felt like taking the plunge and officially move in together, then so be it. But for now, I wanted to date like any other normal couple.

Since I was still a baby vampire, though, Lucian was hesitant about leaving me completely alone. He was afraid I'd attack an innocent bystander, so he'd been staying with me at my apartment since I'd made the decision to leave the club. I personally thought I was good, and continuously pointed out the fact that I'd never even had the urge to attack any of the donors at *Silver Moon,* but Lucian was adamant. It really threw a wrench in my, '*date like normal people*', plans. Just because I was a supernatural creature now, it didn't mean I couldn't still be somewhat normal, right? I mean, I was all for the occasional sleep-over with Lucian, but I still wanted to be able to live a separate, independent life.

This last week had really taken a toll on Lucian. He'd been torn by his need to protect and watch over me and his obligations as the owner of a club and his Consul position. Basically, he'd been neglecting a lot of his responsibilities because there just wasn't enough of him to go around. So much so, that he even decided to hire an assistant to help him get caught up and keep things running smoothly. I hated it for Lucian, but it also presented the perfect opportunity for me to propose a compromise.

Much to my delight, my previous werewolf live-in bodyguard, Aiden, recently decided to work for me permanently. He'd moved back in with his parents after my Becoming, but once I'd explained the situation, he was more than willing to live with me again; at least until I was deemed *safe* to be completely by myself. With my new babysitter lined up, who was more than capable of taking me down if I went blood crazy, and after reminding Lucian of his mounting meeting requests as Louisville's Consul—the vampire version of a local sheriff and counselor, all rolled into one—he reluctantly agreed to let me stay at the apartment with Aiden, while he resumed his duties at *Silver Moon*.

Today was the first day of our new arrangement. Aiden had moved back in the night before and was in the office beneath my apartment with me, helping get everything ready for a smooth re-opening next week. It was the first night since I went from being a human to a vampire that Lucian wasn't by my side, and I'd be lying if I said I didn't miss him. It took everything I had to keep from giving in and asking him to come back, but I kept reminding myself that it was for the best.

We'd been drawn together from the moment we first met by an irresistible attraction. It was so powerful that in the beginning, I was convinced our strange magnetism toward each other could only be the result of some type of crazy vampire power. While I openly admit that I've never felt for anyone else what I feel for Lucian, and that I could easily see us being together for the long haul, my need to get back to some resemblance of my old life and wanting to let our relationship grow slowly, far outweighed those other needs and desires.

Having Aiden there helped. He was as big a part of my life now as Lucian was, and had cemented that role even before I became a vampire. He was like the protective brother I'd never had, but always wanted. I knew having him there would help keep the raw need that I felt for Lucian in check, while also making sure I didn't *vamp out* in front of any unsuspecting humans.

I still didn't think that would be a problem, though. So far, I'd managed to only consume bagged blood and Lucian's. Lucian was right when he tried to explain to me when I was a human how sex and blood-taking were closely related, as I've yet to partake in the first without wanting the other. I've been able to resist a few times, but while in the moment, it was hard not to bite down and drink my fill. Lucian even struggled with restraint in that department, so we usually both ended up with half-healed bite marks by the time we were finished—not that I'm complaining.

Lucian's blood, while still delicious, wasn't as nourishing as human blood. He claimed vampires couldn't survive off another vampire's blood alone; that we had to have human blood to give our own bodies what they needed. I wanted to call bullshit on that, but I wasn't willing to test it. Especially since I could drink human blood from bags, and I didn't have to actually bite anyone. Just the thought of biting into a stranger's skin made me queasy. Maybe I wouldn't feel the same way once I actually did it, but I wasn't willing to test that theory either.

Although werewolf blood was supposed to be bland compared to a human or a vampire's, we could also survive from drinking it—that's why I wanted to call bullshit on not being able to survive on vampire blood. How were we able to live off another species' blood like werewolves, but not our own? I would much rather gorge myself on Lucian every day than heat up a glass of human blood in the microwave.

I was also told that werewolves weren't usually willing donors for vampires; there was too much bad blood—pun intended—there. There was a long history between the two species, which members of both parties refused to discuss with me. Every time I asked questions about it, I was told the past was in the past, and all that mattered now was that they got along . . . mostly. Since vampires lived so long, there were many of them that still carried a grudge and treated werewolves as second-class citizens.

Food was another disappointment for me. While it smelled absolutely amazing with my new heightened senses, the taste of it was not. It was very deceptive for food to smell so good but taste so dull. I could tell what I was eating, but my taste buds just weren't the same anymore. They only had one craving now and that was for blood.

"I've called three times, and you're still not open. When are you coming back?" The male voice on the other end of the phone let out an exasperated groan. "This is Mark Taylor," he paused, "again. I'll try back in a few more days." The voicemail ended, and I shook my head as I deleted it and replaced the handset on the base.

Mark Taylor wasn't an existing client and so far, he hadn't said why he needed my services as a private investigator on any of his three voicemails, or given a number for me to call him back. This particular one was left last week, so I was sure there would be at least one more in my voice mailbox before I got through the rest of them. It did make me curious to find out why he felt like it was so urgent to speak with me but wouldn't leave a call back number.

I sighed with relief as I looked at the flashing number on my phone. I only had nine more voicemails to go through. When I'd sat down early that morning, there was almost a hundred, so to finally be in the single digits was satisfying. After that, though, was the hard part; calling everyone back. At least I didn't have any pending cases that I had to worry about. I could never thank Aiden and his best friend, Jimmy, enough for taking care of my business while I stayed under the radar. They had shut the office down for any new clients and closed the cases I had open involving insurance claims, adoption records, and tracking down MIA spouses to serve divorce papers to.

I had several clients on retainer for processing background checks on new hires, but I insisted on continuing those myself. If nothing else, to keep my sanity. There was no way I could've survived doing nothing the last two months besides hanging out at the club. And since processing background checks were done electronically, I figured it was safe for me to handle those personally.

During my confinement to *Silver Moon,* Lucian and I also had to put more dates on hold, for obvious reasons, so we still only had the one official date under our belts. We'd basically been living together for the past two months, but since I couldn't be trusted in public, we hadn't been able to go on any more dates. Now that I was somewhat stable in my vampireness and wouldn't turn into a blood-crazed maniac on the loose if we did go out, we were going to try it.

Tomorrow night, we were planning a simple and quick trip to the movies and then back to my place. Baby steps. We were originally supposed to go tonight, but since there was still so much that needed to be done around the office in preparation for re-opening, I'd asked if we could postpone until tomorrow night. It was probably going to take Aiden and me all day to do the call-backs from voicemails, schedule new appointments, and update files.

A trip to my grandparent's house was another item on my list of things to do before the re-opening next week. I hadn't seen them since the night Malus and Jessica kidnapped me, and I felt terrible for that. I'd promised them before I left that night that I'd be back soon, and two and a half months later, I hadn't kept my word. Now that I could safely be around them again, I planned on spending an entire day with them soon.

They lived about forty-five minutes south in a town known to the locals as E-Town. My grandparents didn't know anyone who lived in Louisville besides me, so I didn't have to worry about them finding out about the office being closed. They'd raised me after my parents were presumed dead when they disappeared during a hiking trip when I was eight, so I despised lying to them. But I tried to ease my conscience by simply omitting the details. I blamed my prolonged absence on being extremely busy—which I had been. I just let her assume that I'd been busy with my job, instead of learning how to be a vampire.

My cell phone rang, and I smiled when I picked it up; my grandmother was calling. She was probably checking to make sure I wasn't going to cancel our plans that weekend.

"Hello?" I happily answered.

"Riley?" My smile faltered. I could tell something wasn't right.

"Mamaw, what's wrong? Are you and Papaw okay?"

"We're fine. Honey, it's Jeremy." My heart leapt. My cousin Jeremey, who lived in Indianapolis, was supposed to be coming down for a week-long visit.

"Was he in a wreck?" I asked numbly.

"No," she said, on the verge of crying. "He got in last night."

Confused, I asked, "So, what happened?"

It took her a moment before she answered, "He went for a jog this morning through the woods and was attacked." She began sobbing. "He was taken to the hospital, and we don't know if he's going to make it."

Who in the hell would be out in those woods? And who would've attacked him? Crime like that just didn't happen where they lived. Jeremy always stayed with his dad, who lived one town even farther south than where our grandparents lived. It was really more of a small community than a town. Besides the occasional theft and run-away farm animals, there wasn't much that happened there. "Do they have someone in custody?"

"No. There isn't anyone to arrest."

I was really confused now. If he was attacked so severely that he was rushed to the hospital, it had to be by a person. There were bobcats and coyotes where they lived, but it was doubtful that either one would've attacked Jeremy. Bobcat sightings were rare because they avoided humans, and coyotes usually tucked tail and ran if they came across one. "I don't understand."

"He was staying at his dad's house and went out for a morning jog. If Brian hadn't been outside and heard the commotion, I'm afraid it would've been so much worse. He ran back there and scared it off before he could see what it was." Jeremy's dad, Brian, was my Mom's brother, and were the only two children my grandparents had.

"What do you mean, what it was?"

"It was some kind of animal, but going by the bite and scratch marks it's too big to be anything from around here. Riley, they said the bite marks looked like it came from something the size of a grizzly bear."

I could feel the blood drain from my face. We didn't have bears here, but I knew something else that could've been big enough.

My grandmother continued, "I don't know much more than that right now. Our county hospital couldn't handle his injuries, so they took him to Louisville."

"When are you coming up to the hospital?"

"As soon as your grandfather gets back. He went into town this morning before I got the phone call."

I'd been trying to persuade them for years to get cellphones for emergencies, but they were stubborn and didn't want to learn new technology.

"I'll head over to the hospital now."

"Okay. We'll be up there as soon as your grandfather gets back," she promised.

"Be careful, I love you."

"I love you, too, dear."

I hung up the phone and forced myself not to cry. My only cousin, my constant childhood companion, had been attacked by a werewolf.

CHAPTER 2

J eremy and I had always been close growing up, despite the three-year age difference. As children we were inseparable, especially after I lost my parents. Jeremy would stay the entire summer with our grandparents, and we would spend our days exploring their thirty-acre mini farm.

As we grew older, and Jeremy started high school, we slowly began spending more time apart. He was the star quarterback of the high school football team and had a different girlfriend every month. When he wasn't occupied with football, or girls, he hung out with his jock friends. I had developed my own close friendship with Hattie, who lived down the road from my grandparent's house, and we stayed busy admiring all of Jeremy's friends and wondering why no one ever asked us out.

But through all of that, Jeremy and I still managed to make time for each other, and I was sad when he graduated high school and moved away for college. I didn't stay lonely for long, though, because no sooner had Jeremy left town, then I was suddenly bombarded with date requests from several of the boys at school. Jeremy would never admit to it, but I was pretty sure he'd threatened all the guys to stay away from me. It was too much of a coincidence that they'd barely even talked to me, but as soon as Jeremy was out of the picture, I had to screen my calls and field dinner and a movie requests.

Jeremy went to college on a football scholarship and played all four years he attended. He didn't go on to the NFL, but he did graduate with a marketing degree that he put to use right after college. His parents divorced after he graduated high school, and his mom moved to Indianapolis. She gave Jeremy a guilt trip about never seeing him, so he decided to move there also and had been working and living there ever since. He still went down to visit his dad and our grandparents for holidays and the occasional weekend, but every summer he would take a full week off work to stay with his dad. Jeremy and I both stayed so busy that we didn't see each other much when he came for visits, but we managed to stay in contact through social media and texting.

"We're here." Aiden pulled me out of my trance.

I nodded and gave him a half-hearted smile before getting out the Jeep. It was the first time he'd spoken since we'd gotten into the vehicle. Aiden hadn't meant to eavesdrop on the conversation with my grandmother, but when you have supernatural hearing, it just kind of happens. After hanging up with her, he was in my office in a matter of seconds.

As soon as I took one look at him, I broke-down. His arms immediately embraced me, and I cried as I told him what happened, and my suspicions about what his attacker was. When

I finally calmed down, he left me to collect myself, while he called Lucian and explained to him what was going on.

Lucian was going to track down Avery and discuss the situation with him. Aiden and Lucian both agreed that if a werewolf did attack Jeremy, it couldn't have been one from around here. They knew all the shifters in a several county radius, and none of them would have attacked a human. Once Lucian had Avery filled in, he was going to meet us at the hospital.

I halted outside the emergency room entrance. I could already smell the blood, and it caught me off guard. I'd known I would have to deal with the scent at the hospital, but being so worried about Jeremy, I had completely forgotten to prepare myself for the onslaught of the aroma. It was a good thing I still had on my sunglasses to protect my eyes from the sun because I could feel them change.

I took a deep breath, closed my eyes, and focused. I could do this. I'd already had one bag of blood that morning to satiate the hunger, and I was there for Jeremy—who was laying in one of those rooms in critical condition. They bled back to normal, and I sighed in relief. This was going to be my biggest test since becoming a vampire, and I had to be strong.

"You okay to do this?" Aiden, who was patiently standing next to me, asked.

Lucian hadn't exaggerated when he said the sun was painful to our eyes. But Aiden and I stood under a covered walkway that filtered out most of the sunlight. I removed my glasses, so I could show him I was ready, "Yes."

He nodded, and we both walked into the hospital together. Just as I had anticipated, the smell grew stronger with each step we took into the building. We stopped at the information desk for his room number and was surprised when we were told to go the emergency room. I'd expected him to be in ICU, but the attendant said his room wasn't ready yet.

As we waited to be buzzed into the ER, Aiden leaned down and whispered, "If anything happens, just act like you're upset." I glanced up at him with a raised eyebrow. Aiden smirked, "I can *console* you," he winked, "as you bury your face in my chest."

Enlightenment dawned on me. "Ah, good idea," I agreed. Knowing that if I couldn't control my vampire traits, I could simply hide them by having Aiden comfort me, made me feel a little easier with what I was about to face.

The door made a sound and opened on its own. As we walked past the curtained rooms trying to find Jeremy's room number, I tried to breathe shallow breaths. I hadn't been around so much blood since my Becoming, and it was calling to me, drawing me in and causing my throat to burn with wanton need. I knew I wouldn't bite anyone—the thought of biting someone other than Lucian made my stomach turn, and not in a good way—but I *was* worried that the hunger would cause my new fangs to make an appearance or my eyes to glow.

I took it one step at a time and managed to resist my urges until we finally found the curtained room where my cousin was being kept. I was even more relieved that none of the nurses questioned us about our relationship to Jeremy. Sometimes, they only allowed family members in the emergency room to see patients, and while I wouldn't have any problems, Aiden would. And I needed him there to get a good look at the wounds. Aiden would be able to easily tell if our predator actually was a werewolf, as I suspected, or something else.

I pulled the curtain to one side to step through and gasped. My grandmother had told me on the phone his injuries were life threatening, but nothing could have prepared me for what I saw. The sheet was covering him up to his waist, so I didn't know how bad the injuries were on his legs, but his chest and arms had been savagely mauled. Thick gauze bandages were wrapped around his waist, chest, both arms, and scalp, and the entire left side of his face was swollen, with the beginning stages of nasty bruises forming.

Blood was soaking through some of the bandages, painting a stark difference against the off-white gauze. It was hard not to notice, but for some reason it didn't call to me like the rest of the blood I'd been smelling had. I shrugged it off. My concern and worry over Jeremy must have outweighed and eradicated any temptation the blood should've had on me.

"I'm going to look under the bandages quickly before anyone comes in," Aiden hesitated, "is that going to be okay with you?"

I nodded and followed Aiden's suit by talking in hushed tones, "I'm not even tempted."

Aiden gave me a strange look before swiftly beginning his task. I watched with a mixture of anxiety and apprehension as he carefully moved each bandage, one at a time, to examine the wounds. He kept his face blank, not giving away any of the conclusions he was coming to. While he focused on that, I concentrated on listening for signs that someone was about to enter our curtained room. One of the many benefits of being a vampire that I enjoyed was the ability to multitask on a whole new level. I could have a conversation with someone, while simultaneously listening in and knowing what was going on in the room next to me.

"Well," he began as he secured the last bandage back in place, "it was definitely a werewolf."

Relief flooded through me, even though I didn't know why. I guess in my mind, I thought if it was a werewolf, we could track down and punish him or her for doing this to my cousin. But, if Jeremy did survive this, there was a very good chance he would become a werewolf himself, and it was something he'd never asked for.

Amy, the girl who was kidnapped along with me two months ago, only had one bite and was now a werewolf, but according to Aiden, others had been mauled to near death and stayed human. They weren't sure why some turned and some didn't. They've even tossed around the idea that some people could be immune to the werewolf gene. The only thing they did know for sure was that the virus came from their saliva and was only present when they were in their wolf form.

"Do you think he'll turn?"

Aiden sighed and looked down at Jeremy. "It's too early to tell. He was only attacked a few hours ago. The virus hasn't had enough time to alter his DNA and progress his healing."

"When will we know?"

He didn't hesitate with an answer, "It usually takes about twenty-four hours for the virus to bond and change someone's DNA. A person can't shift until their first full moon, but once the virus has made those initial alterations, healing begins to happen at a quickened pace, and the body begins emitting a faint scent of werewolf. It won't be a full-blown werewolf scent like you can smell from me, though, until after the first shift."

I knew most of what Aiden had said from my experience with Amy. The same day I had been turned into a vampire, Amy had been bitten by a werewolf. She had the same musky scent that werewolves had, but it was a diluted, toned-down version. It wasn't until after she shifted for the first time that her scent was as strong as the rest of them.

"What if he is?" I asked. "How do we explain his rapid healing to the doctors?"

Aiden snorted and focused his attention on me. "There's enough supernatural doctors and nurses here that will make sure it stays quiet."

"Are you sure?"

"Trust me, this isn't the first werewolf or vampire attack that's made it to the hospital. As soon as they realize what they're dealing with, they'll remove all humans from his care."

"Good." I nodded, reassured. "If he is, then that's the last thing we need—for there to be suspicion about what he is and him being thrown in the spotlight."

Aiden put his hands in his jean pockets, "We've been covering our tracks for centuries, so we've gotten pretty good at it. More than likely they'll blame this on a bear."

I crossed my arms, "But we don't have bears around here."

He gave me a pointed look, "How much you want to bet there will be an article in tomorrow's paper about bear sightings near your cousin's house?"

"Someone will call in fake sightings to cover this up?" It made sense, but I was surprised at the lengths they would go to make sure the attack was covered up.

"I know you're still new to this, but secrecy is everything to us, and we'll stop at almost nothing to keep it that way. That's the one thing most supernaturals agree on."

"Well, I guess at least vampires and werewolves can agree on something."

He shook his head. "Not just those two. *All* the supes. But there's usually a few in each of the groups that think we'd be better off out in the open." Aiden gave me another pointed look. "Like Malus."

"All?" I asked hesitantly. I'd never asked, and apparently, it'd never come up, but I was under the impression that there were only vampires, werewolves, and humans.

A strange expression crossed his face. "You don't know about the others?"

I started to ask just what else what out there, but the tingling spread down my arms, right before I heard two voices near the curtain. One I recognized instantly, but the other was unfamiliar. The curtain was pulled back to reveal my uncle, Jeremy's father, and a tall man in a doctor's coat. The doctor had short dark hair, high cheek bones, framed by a strong jawline, warm hazel eyes, and as with most vampires, he was very attractive.

"Uncle Brian!" I rushed over and embraced my uncle in a hug, which he generously returned.

"Hey. I'm glad you came," he said as we released each other.

"Are you kidding? How couldn't I?"

He gave me a smile, which didn't quite reach his eyes. "I know." My uncle gave me a kiss on the cheek before he walked next to Jeremy's bedside and took his hand.

I looked to the doctor, who seemed genuinely surprised to see another vampire and a werewolf standing there. "How is he?"

"Well," he cleared his throat, quickly recovering from his shock, "considering the wounds he's endured, very well. The animal narrowly missed all organs and major arteries. He did lose a lot of blood and while his injuries are severe, none of them appear to be fatal."

I glanced at Brian. My usually cheerful and joking uncle was wallowing in uncertainty and grief. His graying hair was messy, and his clothes were ruffled and unkept; the attack must have happened before he'd had the chance to get ready for the day. "So, he's going to make it?" I wanted to make sure I understood what the doctor was saying. If Jeremy wasn't infected with the werewolf virus, I needed to know that he wouldn't die from this.

"I believe so," he paused, "he's still in critical condition, and there will be a long road ahead of him with physical therapy, but it looks hopeful. We're actually ready to move him to the ICU now."

"Thank you, doctor."

"My pleasure. I'll be in charge of Mr. Williams while he's here at the hospital, so if you have any questions or concerns," he raised an eyebrow, silently sending Aiden and myself a message about which type of concerns he was referring to, "just ask for Dr. Martin."

"Thank you for everything," my uncle chimed in. He'd finally taken his eyes from Jeremy and gave Dr. Martin the full extent of his mournful gaze.

The doctor nodded. "The nurses should be here in a few minutes to transport him upstairs." With that said, Dr. Martin left, pulling the curtain closed behind him.

"I don't believe we've met," my uncle said to Aiden as he extended his hand over the hospital bed.

My uncle was a good man. He was a hard worker, kind, and loved his family, but he didn't handle tragedy or emotions very well. He was old school and didn't think it was proper for a man to cry, even under circumstances such as this. By reverting to social niceties, he was trying to distract himself and avoid his own grief.

Aiden reached out instantly to shake his hand. "No, we haven't. I'm Aiden. It's a pleasure to meet you, Mr. Williams."

"Pleasure's all mine." Uncertainty filled my uncle's face as he glanced at me. Cleary, he'd been talking to Mamaw, who in true Mamaw-fashion, had relayed the gossip that Riley had a boyfriend named Lucian. He obviously thought Lucian was who he should've been shaking hands with.

"Aiden," I quickly stepped into the conversation and put a gentle hand on Aiden's arm, "works with me. He was there when Mamaw called and told me about Jeremy, so he drove me over here."

"Oh." A genuine smile returned, replacing his confusion, as he let go of Aiden's hand.

"Well, if you'll excuse me," Aiden started toward the curtain, "I'm going to step outside and make a few phone calls." That was code for: I'm going to call Lucian and Avery and tell them what we found out.

"Okay. I shouldn't be too much longer. Since Jeremy will probably be out for a while, and they're getting ready to move him, I'm not going to stay. I'll meet you at the car."

Aiden left, leaving me and my uncle alone, which gave me the opportunity to question him about what happened. "So, where exactly was he was attacked?"

My uncle cleared his throat, "He was jogging on the path behind the house. He'd only made it about thirty feet into the woods when I heard him," he looked down at the floor, trying to compose himself, "scream."

I went over and hugged him. "Did you see what attacked him?"

"No, by the time I got there, it'd already left." He quickly swiped away the tears that had trickled down his cheeks. "They're saying more than likely it was a bear." It didn't escape my notice that he didn't sound totally convinced by that theory.

"I know." I released him, "But even if it was a bear, they'll want to euthanize an animal that's attacked a human."

"Yeah, they need to get that son of a bitch before it attacks anyone else," he said with venom and disdain.

I was a little taken aback by that statement. Not so much in what he said, but how he said it. He was giving me the distinct vibe that he didn't believe it was a bear attack at all. But since it was clearly some type of animal that did attack Jeremy, it made me wonder what my uncle *did* think happened. Surely, he didn't suspect the creature that was actually responsible? Unless . . . I quickly discarded that thought. There was no way he knew about supernaturals, right? "Would you mind if I go down to your house and look around? Just to make sure the police and wildlife department didn't overlook anything."

"I don't know what you could find that they missed, but since I'm sure whatever did this to Jeremy is long-gone by now, I don't see what it would hurt. You always have been good at investigating things." He laughed, "I guess that's why you chose the career you did."

I gave him a warm smile. "Thanks. I'll go straight there when I leave. Do you need me to pick up anything for you while I'm down there?"

"No, I'm fine. I'm going to stay here until Laura gets back and Jeremy is settled in his room. Then I'll go home and get changed and grab some stuff, so I can stay here with him . . . at least for tonight."

I frowned as I realized I hadn't seen Laura, his ex-wife, and Jeremy's mother there. I wasn't very fond of her, or really I should say that she wasn't very fond of me. She and my mother never got along when I was a child, and she took that out on me. I couldn't remember a time when she had ever been genuinely nice to me. Her contempt for members of his family was one of the many reasons which led to their divorce. I was so thankful that Jeremy took more after Brian than he did Laura. "Where is she?"

"She's in the cafeteria getting some coffee."

What perfect timing for my visit. Any time I could avoid Laura, I did. "Well, I'll see you in a few hours then."

"You be careful, okay? We don't need two of you up here in this hospital."

I smiled and gave him another hug. "Don't worry, I'll be back before you know it."

I took one last look at Jeremy before leaving. It made me sick to think someone could do that to another person. From what I understood about werewolves, they had urges and instincts while in their wolf-form but knew exactly what was going on and what they were doing. So, whoever did this to my cousin, had to have done it intentionally. I hurried my steps, anxious to rendezvous with Lucian and Avery, so we could head down to my uncle's house and see what we could find.

CHAPTER 3

S ince there was still so much that needed to be done before the re-opening, Aiden offered to stay behind and work on getting some of it finished, so I could help with the investigation into my cousin's attack. We went back to the office after leaving the hospital, where Lucian and Avery were already waiting. Aiden went inside to start working, while the rest of us piled into Lucian's Land Rover and headed down to my uncle's house.

My uncle lived in Glendale, which was a neighboring small town of E-Town, where my grandparents lived. It was known for good restaurants, antiques, and arts and crafts. They had a festival each October which drew thousands of people to the tiny community who couldn't get enough of the craft booths and samples of southern cooking at its finest, including my grandmother and me. It was a yearly tradition for us to kick off our Christmas shopping together at the festival.

Lucian was driving, I was in the front passenger seat, and Avery was in the back behind Lucian. After driving most of the way there in silence, I turned around, so I could ask a few questions that had been bothering me. "Lucian said he knew it couldn't be anyone in your pack. Why is that?"

"Because no one in our pack would have attacked a human," he huffed.

"Okay," I drew out the word. I wasn't implying that they would, because I did believe them when they said a member of the local pack wouldn't have attacked someone. I'd met several members of the pack, and if the rest of them were like any of the ones I'd already met, I would never think they were capable of anything like that—on purpose. I just wanted to know what made them so sure that it couldn't have been one of theirs, and that it couldn't have been an accident.

"And none of us would have shifted down there," Avery added.

"Why?" I knew werewolves had no choice but to shift during the full moon; Aiden had mentioned something about the moon calling to their inner beasts and that they couldn't resist it. But any other time of the month they could shift at will. And like vampires, strong emotions could let their true nature slip out unintentionally.

"We fear exposure. And because of that fear, we don't feel comfortable changing anywhere other than on pack land."

"What if they get caught out somewhere else and something happens?"

Avery sighed and crossed his arms, seemingly annoyed. He was the head of Lucian's security team at *Silver Moon,* and he also just happened to be second in command of the local werewolf pack. The same pack that Aiden and pretty much every werewolf in a several county radius belonged to. I didn't know much about Avery, just a few pieces of information that I'd picked up here and there, like the fact that he wasn't born a werewolf. He was in the military when he was younger, until he came back from an overseas deployment as a newly created werewolf. He'd been stationed at Fort Knox, which was also a neighboring city of E-Town, so he joined the local pack and moved to Louisville.

Other than that, Avery was a mystery to me. Just from my limited experience around him, I knew he ran the security team like a well-oiled, disciplined machine. Even if I hadn't overheard about his military beginnings, it would have been easy to guess. I'd also noticed that Avery became aggravated easily, especially when asked multiple questions about anything. He wasn't much of a talker and usually stuck to simple answers. I was the type of person that questioned everything and almost always had a follow up ready, so needless to say, I had a reputation of getting on Avery's nerves over the last couple of months.

"You might as well get used to it, Avery, and answer her questions. I'm sure Riley's full of them, and you're stuck in a vehicle with her." Lucian smirked amusingly.

Avery snorted with disapproval, but answered regardless with a pointed glare, "In the unfortunate circumstance that we are elsewhere, then we obviously improvise, but that's irrelevant. The simple fact is that no one in our pack would have attacked him, regardless of if they turned in front of him, or came across him in their wolf form."

I turned back around in my seat and thought about that for a few minutes. Jeremy's injuries were extensive, so it wasn't like he only had an accidental swipe from a set of claws as a warning to stay away, or one bite from an inadvertent startling. He was mauled. I had a gut feeling that Avery was right, and there was no way it could have been a member of their pack, but as Jeremy's family member, I had to question him about it, all the same.

"Right here, on the left." I directed Lucian. My uncle's home was about a mile away from the main street that ran through Glendale. It was a newer brick, ranch-style house that sat back a good distance from the road. He had neighbors on both sides, but they were spread out far enough that you still felt like you had some privacy. A large patch of woods occupied a huge amount of space behind all the houses on this stretch of the road, which only added to the feel of seclusion these homes offered. And unfortunately for my cousin, allowed a werewolf to remain hidden until he ran right into it.

Lucian stopped at the end of the driveway, directly in front of the storage shed that sat cattycornered to the house. We all exited the vehicle, and a wave of exhaustion made me stop in my tracks. When I was a human, summer was my favorite time of the year. I loved the heat, and my idea of the perfect day was laying by a pool, soaking up some Vitamin D. Now that I was a vampire, I detested the summer and couldn't wait until it was over. It was the end of July, and the sun was bearing down on me with a vengeance. My sunglasses helped to shield my eyes, but there was only so much I could do about the sun's rays that had an unfortunate draining effect on my body. It basically felt like I had the flu anytime I had to go out during the day. And the sunnier it was outside, the worse I felt.

I took a deep breath and pushed through the exhaustion. I'd already learned in my limited time as a vampire that if I could just force myself to keep going through the initial wave of fatigue, it would get more manageable the longer I had to be out in the direct sunlight. The guys had already started toward the backyard, so I caught up with them and stopped Avery before we got any farther. We weren't exactly at the top of each other's *'people I really like list'* and, actually, I'd be surprised if Avery even had one of those. He seemed to like Lucian okay, but that was about it. But since we were going be working closely to figure out how this happened to my cousin, then I needed to keep things civil and it wasn't starting out so well.

"Avery," I began, "I just want to apologize now because I know until we figure this out, I'm going to be asking you a lot of questions, and more than likely, it's going to irritate you." I paused and shifted my weight from one leg to the other, "I just want to make sure that what happened to my cousin doesn't happen to anyone else, and to do that I need to know as much about you guys as I possibly can. I'll try to keep most of my questions reserved for Aiden, but I know I'm going to have to come to you for some of them."

There, I'd said my piece. Now it was time to see if it would only piss him off even more.

He stood there a moment, staring at me. Irritation laced his expression, but was soon replaced by something else. Was that appraisal? It was hard to tell with him. "I appreciate your honesty and dedication." He reached up and rubbed the back of his hairless head. "I want the same thing you do, so I'll try to have a little more patience." He dropped his hand, "Now, which way do we go?"

I let out a sigh of relief and pointed the way toward the section of trees where the path should have been. I felt better.

At least Avery and I had an understanding, and hopefully, we could figure this out before anyone else got hurt. Avery may be standoffish and reserved, but I knew he would put forth every effort in tracking down Jeremy's attacker. I'd seen firsthand his dedication to finding Malus a few months ago, and I knew he would do the same now.

Lucian and I fell behind Avery, walking alongside each other. I dared a glance his way, and Lucian grinned at me approvingly. I'd have given almost anything to see his eyes right then. I was sure if they weren't hidden by sunglasses, they would have looked like sparkling emeralds in the sunlight.

"I wanted to tell you that I'm very proud of you." Lucian beamed.

Confused, I asked, "For what?"

"Aiden told me how well you did at the hospital today."

"Oh, well," I looked ahead to see the distance between Avery and us growing. He was already nearing the tree line where my cousin had been attacked. "I was just so worried about Jeremy that I didn't really think about anything else."

He put an arm around my shoulders, forcing me to stop walking and turn toward him, "Regardless of *how* you kept focused, you still managed to do it. And that's a big accomplishment for a young vampire." He leaned down, giving me a chaste, but tender kiss.

We'd shared hundreds of them over the past few months, some more tame than others, and every single one of them still managed to affect me. It would be so easy to give in to what my body and my heart craved; to do little else that took me out and away from his arms. But luckily, I still had my head that kept me grounded and reminded me that I had a life to live outside of Lucian.

Sensing the way my breath hitched and how my heart rate increased from his touch, Lucian pulled back and smirked, "I love the way you react to me."

Sometimes, I hated that I couldn't hide anything from his heightened senses, but at least now it was a two-way street. *My* new and improved senses could hear how his body reacted the exact same way to me. I gave him a knowing grin, "Ditto."

"Found it." Avery's voice drifted from inside the woods. Lucian and I both ran toward the area where his voice had come from, and I scolded myself for getting sidetracked . . . again. Lucian always managed to distract me, no matter what situation we found ourselves in. I knew it wasn't intentional, but it was aggravating all the same. And just another reason why I wanted to make sure I maintained a little bit of distance between us, regardless of how I felt about him.

Avery was only about thirty feet inside the tree line. Even blindfolded, I would have been able to find the spot. There was blood splashed everywhere, and so many different human scents it was a little disorienting. I only recognized two of them as my cousin and uncle, so I assumed the rest belonged to police officers, paramedics, and possibly animal control.

The first responders had clearly trampled through most of the area. The woods weren't overgrown through this part and only had ankle-high weeds and tree sprouts on either side of the five-foot wide dirt path, but most of it was now flattened and covered in dried blood. It was hard to tell if the blood in those outlining areas was from the attack, or the result of all those people accidentally tracking it there while they tried to save Jeremy's life.

The trees created a canopy and blocked most of the direct sunlight, so the main pool of blood in the middle of the path hadn't had time to dry completely. That must have been where Jeremy had lain until the EMS technicians were able to move him. Avery was already on the opposite side of it, facing me and Lucian with his eyes closed and breathing deeply.

"Riley," Lucian nostrils flared, "there's something off about his blood."

"What do you mean?" The smell of the blood was overwhelming to me, but like at the hospital, I wasn't necessarily drawn to Jeremy's blood like I probably should've been.

"It's been quite a long time since I've come across it, but it's almost as if . . .," he trailed off.

"Almost as if what?"

"Nothing." He shook his head. "I'm sure it's nothing." He started to make his way toward Avery. "Let's just focus on finding this werewolf."

Even though I wasn't ready to drop to my knees and lap it up, it was blood, nonetheless, and hard to focus on anything other than it resting in a giant puddle right in front of me. I'd drank a glass of it before I went to the hospital, but being around so much of it there and now here, was starting to wear on my restraint. I decided to get a little distance between myself and the source of my affliction, so I could concentrate. I needed to try and help Avery and Lucian find any werewolf scents, but standing there like a statue with drool hanging out of my mouth certainly wasn't going to help anyone.

I tore my eyes away from the blood and maneuvered my Converses into the woods, careful to avoid any of the dried splotches of blood scattered everywhere or any signs of poison ivy. I'd always been allergic to it and I didn't want to take the chance that becoming a vampire hadn't cured my reaction to the plant. The last thing I needed to deal with right then was an itchy rash.

When I was several feet off of the path, I stopped in my tracks. I drew in a deep breath, "I think I smell two werewolves right here."

"Those are just the two wildlife agents," Avery said without looking up. He had also moved into the woods, about thirty feet away from me, but was on all fours, his face only a few inches from the ground.

Lucian was already at Avery's side, with his sunglasses in his hand, eyes closed, and inhaling the scent himself. "How strange. It's faint, but definitely there."

"Too faint to track," Avery added. "It won't be long before it's gone altogether."

Some vampires had extra abilities, like my gift of being able to sense when other vampires were near. Lucian was able to catch glimpses of what people were thinking if they were really focused and concentrating on something, or if the thoughts were accompanied by a strong emotion. Since nothing had been spoken out loud about finding a scent, I assumed Lucian had picked something up from Avery, so I made my way over there and squatted down next to them, closing my eyes and breathing in deeply again. They were right. It was very faint, but there was definitely a musky and unfamiliar werewolf scent. I opened my eyes and looked to Lucian with a raised eyebrow, silently asking what our next step was.

His eyes had changed from their normal bright green, to the silvery vampire iridescence, with slivers of emerald cascading through them. "I agree, Avery. It's very suspicious, but I'm going to follow it as far as I can and look for anything the werewolf might have left behind." He stood and began searching the area. Avery followed suit, and I watched, mesmerized as they both gracefully stalked through the woods in search of their prey.

I wanted to follow, but uncertainty held me back. My instincts were screaming at me to let my vampire out and track the werewolf with them, but my mind was reminding me that I still had no clue how to do any of that. I'd spent the last two months learning how to tame and hide my vampire instincts and characteristics, not to embrace and use them. Honestly, I still didn't even know what all I was capable of.

Maybe that was another reason I was hesitant about remaining locked away in Lucian's basement apartment. Was my subconscious really wanting a chance to explore my new abilities, since so far I'd only been taught how to suppress them? I knew Lucian hadn't been doing that intentionally, because it was far more important for me to learn how to hide and control them first, but that didn't mean I wasn't and hadn't been curious about what I could do now.

I filed that thought away. There were more important things to worry about at the moment. I focused on the two men venturing farther away from me and further into the woods with a sense of longing. My gums began aching, begging for me to release my teeth and chase after them. Between the provoking smell of blood and the urge to pursue the werewolf with Lucian and Avery, I knew my restraint wouldn't last long. Everything out there in the woods was enticing my vampire nature and demanding that I let go and embrace it.

I shook my head to clear it. As much as I wanted to find out what I was capable of, the thought of doing just that scared the shit out of me. What if I let go and couldn't rein it back in? With equal parts reluctance and raw willpower, I turned my back on the guys and my instincts and slowly trudged back to Lucian's vehicle. I wouldn't be much use to them anyway, even if I did go after them. I didn't have experience using my heightened senses, and Avery, being a werewolf, had a much more advanced sniffer than I did. And Lucian knew what he was looking for, whereas I didn't.

While I waited for Avery and Lucian to come back to the vehicle, it gave me time to think about things. Like if Jeremy was a werewolf now, how was he going to handle it? What would my grandparents think if they knew they didn't have human grandchildren anymore? They only had two, and one was a vampire and the other possibly a werewolf.

And how would he hide the secret from his friends and family? As far as I knew, he was single at the moment, but eventually he'd meet someone, and he'd either have to hide it from her, or tell her about it. Unless he ended up with another werewolf, which would probably be for the best. I couldn't imagine having that conversation with your spouse when your children suddenly turned furry during the full moon.

Children.

I hadn't even thought about that. I'd never really been in a hurry to get married and have kids, but when imagining my future, I had always envisioned at least one or two children in it. Now, I wasn't so sure. I knew vampires could have kids, but for some reason it was difficult to conceive. Vampire children went through the transition from mostly human to vampire somewhere between the ages of sixteen and twenty-five, but I wasn't sure exactly how that worked. All I knew for certain was that they went through their Becoming around adulthood, which was similar to the transition that I went through when Lucian turned me. Ellie, a bartender at *Silver Moon* and also a vampire, had explained a little bit about how vampire procreation worked, but I still had so many questions.

I really wished I could use Google to find out about my new life, but unfortunately that only resulted in pages upon pages of myths and movie recommendations. I was actually a little embarrassed at how many times I'd tried to search random questions that came to mind, knowing they wouldn't produce any legit answers, but hoping I could somehow find shreds of the truth hidden in there. We really needed some kind of supernatural Wikipedia.

The sun was beating down on me, making me uncomfortable. Lucian had assured me that I wouldn't feel the heat and cold to the degree that I did as a human, but with the heat index over a hundred degrees today, I was sure as fuck feeling it. A bead of sweat trickled down my back, and I scolded myself for not changing into shorts and flip flops before coming down here. I'd had jeans and shoes on when I went to the hospital, and the last thing I'd been worried about before traveling down to my uncle's house was my wardrobe.

Luckily, I always wore a hair tie on my wrist; a habit from years of having long hair. I bent over, flipping my dirty blonde hair over my head, and wrapped it in a loose bun. My phone vibrated in my back pocket. I forgot I'd switched it over from ringing before I went into the hospital earlier. Hoping it was news about Jeremy, I raised up and answered it quickly without looking at the screen.

"Why haven't you called me? Is he okay? How are you doing?" I grinned at the frantic string of queries from my best friend, Hattie. We'd been friends since elementary school and even though she still lived in E-Town, we stayed in touch and tried to meet up once a month to get lunch and hang out.

I'd had to cancel our lunch dates the last several months— first out of fear that Malus would target her to get to me, and then for her safety after I changed—so it had been a while since I'd seen her. Hearing her normal point-blank hysteria made me realize just how much I missed her.

"Well, hello to you, too." I waited to hear her frustrated sigh on the other end of the line before I answered her questions. "I haven't called you because I went from shock, to making sure he's okay, to trying to figure out what happened all in the couple of hours since I found out about the attack. He's torn up pretty good, but the doctor thinks he's going to be okay. And to answer your last question, I'm doing better now that I've talked to the doctor, and he said Jeremy will make it."

"Thank goodness!" Hattie mimicked my thoughts exactly. "You know how news travels fast around here. It's all over social media. I thought you would've already called me, but I guess I didn't stop to realize that it literally just happened."

I leaned against Lucian's vehicle, "It's okay, Hattie." That was as close to an, I'm sorry, that I'd get from her. I knew she was just worried about Jeremy. Hattie could—and did—get any guy she wanted, but she never stayed with them for long. She was always on the lookout for the perfect man and never failed to find numerous flaws in every guy she dated.

There was only one man that she'd ever wanted, but never pursued, and that was Jeremy. She'd been crushing on him since middle school when we realized boys weren't so gross anymore and some of them were actually cute. She would never talk about it, but it was obvious she had it bad for him. Even now, as adults, she would find ways to ask me how he was and would make sure to stop by my grandparent's house during holidays when he was there.

I hadn't figured out if the reason she never went after Jeremy was because of our friendship, or since he was the one she actually always wanted, if she was scared he would reject her. Either way, as far as I knew, Jeremy was completely clueless about Hattie's feelings toward him all these years.

"I was thinking about going up to see him when I get off work," she said hesitantly. "Will you be there?"

"Probably not that late," I answered honestly. "I've got a ton of work to do at the office, and I'm sure they're going to keep him doped up on pain meds, so I doubt he'll even be awake today." Hattie was silent, so I added, "But don't let that stop you from going there."

"Okay," she said after a moment, "I'll go. You never know, he might be awake. Maybe I'll stop at the local bakery on my way up there and pick him up some of that peanut butter fudge he likes." I smirked knowingly. Some things never changed. "Even if he's not awake yet, I can leave it, and he can eat it when he feels up to it."

"I think he'd like that," I agreed, trying to hide the amusement from my voice.

"But that still doesn't solve the fact that I haven't seen you in months." Hattie's voice went from unsure and considering to stern and accusing. "You promised when that case was over we'd get together, and I know you're done working on it."

I leaned my head back against the Land Rover and looked up at the clear blue sky. I'd somehow managed to avoid this conversation since I'd been turned. I was pretty sure I was ready. I'd done damn good at the hospital today, and I was already planning on visiting my grandparents the coming up weekend, but Lucian would be going with me for added insurance, and I knew that wouldn't fly with Hattie. She would want it to be just the two of us. Maybe I could have Aiden hang out on the other side of the restaurant?

I pushed away from the Land Rover and straightened. I had an idea. "You're right. I'm sorry, Hattie. Why don't you come up to my apartment on Sunday? I can make us some lunch, and we can drink some wine?" And that way, Aiden could either hang out in his room, or downstairs. He would be just a short distance away if things got out of hand.

"Hmm, it has been a while since I've been to your place." She was trying to act like she was thinking about it, but I knew better. I had her at wine. "Okay, fine. But if you bail on me again—"

"I promise I won't cancel," I interrupted. I heard movement in the woods and looked over to see Lucian and Avery emerging from the trees. "Hey, I've got to go. I'm good anytime on Sunday, so just text me and let me know what time you want to come up."

"Okay, I'll let you know soon."

"I can't wait, it's been too long." At least I didn't have to lie about that. "I'll see you then. Be careful driving up to Louisville tonight."

"Hey, wait," she said. "Listen, before you hang up there's something I need to tell you." Hattie hesitated, before she blew out a deep breath. "Just, be careful yourself. I have a bad feeling." My blood suddenly ran cold, and a chill swept over my body. She had only said those words a few times over the years, and every time she had, something bad had happened. From us barely avoiding a fatal collision, to steering clear of a party where a girl was kidnapped and found dead a few days later.

"I will," I managed to say after swallowing hard and ended the call.

"Are you okay?" Lucian came up beside me.

"Yeah," I smiled faintly. "I was just talking to Hattie. She was worried about Jeremy." I didn't see the need to mention what she'd said. Sometimes, I even had a hard time believing how spot on her intuition could be. "What did you find?"

"Unfortunately, nothing helpful. And the fact that his scent is barely there only raises more questions."

Afraid to admit how my inexperience hindered me about scents, but also wanting to know the answer, I reluctantly asked. "And why is that?"

"The werewolf only went through here a few hours ago, so it should have been much stronger. It's like it's been a few days, versus only a few hours."

"And how does that happen?"

"I have a hunch," he ran a frustrated hand through his hair, "but it's so far-fetched that I don't know if I should even say it out loud."

"Might as well." Avery said indifferently. "If your hunch is what I think it is, and it's true, then she'll find out soon enough."

Now I was really curious. I stared at Lucian expectantly. There was no way he couldn't tell me about his hunch now.

"Fine." He gave Avery the side-eye. "There is one supernatural that can and does hide their scent from all the others. It allows them to stay under the radar, and unless they choose to reveal themselves, they appear as any other normal human."

I was glad Aiden had already outed the fact that there were other supernaturals, or I wouldn't have been able to hide the shock from my face. "Okay, so how does that tie in here? Do you think this supe was turned into a werewolf?"

Avery snorted. "These creatures lose their powers if they're turned into a vampire or a shifter, so there's no way that's how the wolf was able to pull this off."

It was easy to tell there was no love lost between Avery and whatever supernatural being they were talking about.

"I agree. I've never heard of one of them retaining powers once the transformation is complete. And as unlikely as it would be, the only explanation is that the werewolf used a potion similar to the one they use to dampen his scent."

Wait. Did he just say potion? As in witches?

Even though I couldn't see Lucian's eyes behind the sunglasses, I could feel them boring into me. He gave a slight nod of his head. "Yes, Riley. We're talking about witches."

Already knowing firsthand that vampires and werewolves existed should've made me impervious to the knowledge that spell-casting witches were a thing as well, but it didn't.

"But what witch in their right mind would work with a shifter?" Avery demanded.

"I can only think of two options—" Lucian began.

"Wait a minute." I held up my hand. "I'm completely lost here. Up until now, I didn't even know witches existed, so can someone please explain why a witch wouldn't work with a shifter?"

Avery's back stiffened. "Because they're just as stuck up, if not worse, than vampires."

I glanced back and forth between the two, waiting for one of them to elaborate.

"While Avery's explanation is a little blunt and vague, he's not wrong. Witches believe they're the superior race, not unlike vampires. But they isolate themselves from all the supernaturals and even go as far as disguising themselves, so we can't even find them, if we wanted to."

"Which we wouldn't," Avery clarified with a scowl.

"Yes," Lucian agreed. "For the most part, we let them keep their secrecy and don't go looking for them."

"For the most part?" I asked as I shifted my feet and swiped the fresh bead of sweat off the back of my neck.

"Witches have powers and can cast spells, so there's always been the occasional vampire or shifter who's tried to harness that for themselves over the centuries."

"Ah, I see. So, to avoid being experimented on by everyone else, they began hiding in plain sight as humans?" I surmised.

Having been the recent target of something similar, I could sympathize with wanting to be invisible to the others.

"Well, yes and no," Lucian said tentatively. "That doesn't really happen very often, especially once it was clear that all their powers and spell-casting abilities vanished once the shifter virus took hold or they went through the Becoming. But the main reason is simply because they don't want to associate with anyone outside of their species.

"They'll sell their services to the humans in the form of psychic readings or charms and spells, but as a general rule, they refuse to work with other supernaturals. Most covens harshly reprimand any witch that does, and even go as far as casting them out of their Coven if caught interacting with another species besides humans. That's why I think if this disappearing scent is related to a witch's spell, there are two possible scenarios. Either the wolf stole the spell from a witch, or he's secretly working for one."

"My bet would be the first." Avery crossed his arms and grunted.

"I don't know. It *would* take something major like die-hard revenge or settling a deep-rooted grudge to get a witch to hire a werewolf." Lucian came closer to me, placing a hand on my arm. "Is there anything you need to tell us about your cousin which would make him the target of a witch?"

"Seriously?" I arched an eyebrow and shrugged Lucian's touch away. "As far as I know, no. Like I said, I didn't even know witches existed until a few minutes ago, so how would I know what Jeremy could even do to piss one off?"

The humming began throbbing in my chest, so I stepped back and took a deep breath to calm down. I was so tired of the smallest things getting me so worked up and having no control over it. In the back of my mind, I knew I shouldn't get so upset over insignificant comments, but my anger had a mind of its own now and didn't care about logic. I'd never been an angry or impulsive person, so trying to cope with these new and strong emotions wasn't easy.

"Sorry." I rubbed my forehead. "I just honestly don't know how a witch would have anything to do with Jeremy."

"It's fine, Riley. I understand your frustration." Lucian smiled gently. "And you really are getting better at reining in your emotions."

"It doesn't feel like it," I admitted.

"Well, you are. And I only asked because there's another side effect of that potion witches use to disguise their scent."

Avery perked up at that comment. Apparently, whatever Lucian was about to say, would also be news to him.

"When they actively use the potion, it also changes the scent of their blood. It's usually only noticeable to a vampire."

My eyes grew wide as I realized what he was insinuating.

"It's been many years since I've come across a witch knowingly, and even more since I've been around their spelled blood, but from what I can remember, their blood isn't enticing. It's almost as if the potion somehow also makes it less alluring to a vampire. But if their blood is spelled and the vampire is familiar with witches, it's practically a dead giveaway to what they are."

That's exactly how I'd reacted to Jeremy's blood earlier that day. I'd assumed it was just because I was so worried about him, but could my non-reaction have been caused by something else? I racked my mind for any indication that Jeremy could be a witch, but nothing stood out. Of course, it didn't really help that I wasn't sure what exactly to look for, but there were no memories of wands, spells, potion-making, or anything else that screamed witch.

I shook my head apologetically. "If he is, then I had no idea."

"Well, then there goes that theory. Witches aren't made, they're born to other witches." Avery walked over and opened the door to Lucian's vehicle. Sweat trickled down the back of his hairless head. At least I wasn't the only one affected by this heat. "But even if the wolf stole it, that still leaves the question of if this was a random attack, or if he was targeted. Either way, we're definitely dealing with a rogue werewolf. That's the only kind that would willingly work with or steal from a witch."

I had to admit that I didn't know much about Jeremy's life in Indianapolis. I had no idea who his friends were, or if he had any enemies. What I did know was that Jeremy was a good guy, and I just couldn't see him getting on the bad side of a werewolf or a witch. But then again, who would've guessed that I'd draw the attention of a vampire? "Okay, so what do we do now?"

"Well, we at least *have* his scent, so we'll know what to look for. Avery is going to alert all the packs in the state that there's possibly a rogue in the area and see if they've had any interactions with one."

Great. With Jeremy unconscious in the hospital and a dead-end here, I was clueless as to what our next move should be. The only thing we had was a scent. If this was a rogue werewolf, then he'd be in hiding. The only thing we could do was sit back and wait for his next move. I wasn't sure if I could do that, but I guess I really didn't have a choice. First, it was homicidal vampires, now we had a rogue werewolf who was possibly working with a witch on the loose. And I was beginning to wonder what else could come our way.

CHAPTER 4

"Hi, George." I waved at the security guard for the gated parking area behind my office and apartment building. It wasn't very large, but it did span the length of my building and several of my neighbor's. It was one of the perks that helped me make the decision of buying this place instead of the others I'd looked at.

"Hello, Ms. Hunter. I'll get the gate open right away."

"George, how many times do I have to tell you, please call me Riley."

He blushed, "Sorry."

George had started working security for the parking lot about six months ago. I still felt twinges of guilt when thinking about him. He was there the night Aiden and Jimmy were attacked in the parking lot by Malus' vampire followers, and I was kidnapped by Jessica. It was a miracle George was still alive. Thankfully, the vampires only knocked George unconscious instead of killing or even drinking from him. I knew there wasn't anything I could've done to prevent it, but if they hadn't been after me then George never would've been in harm's way, so I still felt responsible for what happened to him.

"Thanks, George." I smiled and waved again as I drove through the gate. He usually worked nights, but recently it seemed like he was working around the clock, and I never knew when he'd be there. That was fine with me, though, because George seemed to always put a smile on my face. He was normally so polite and a perfect gentleman that it made me wonder why he would choose a job like security. It didn't seem to fit his shy personality.

I also wondered if he'd ever really had a serious girlfriend. He was cute enough; about my age with brown curly hair and dark-brown eyes. He was a little on the pudgy side, but had one of those round baby faces and dimpled cheeks that made him appear younger than he really was. I had a feeling his timid and bashful demeanor routinely placed him more in a girl's friend zone than potential boyfriend material.

I parked next to the stairs that led up to my apartment and just sat there for a moment. I was totally exhausted. Actually, exhausted didn't even begin to describe how I felt. It wasn't a physical exhaustion, but an emotional one, which was just as tiring. Even though there was still plenty of work to do in the office, there was no way I was up to the task that evening. It had just been too long of a day.

Lucian dropped me off at the office after we came back from my uncle's house in Glendale. Aiden and I worked for a few more hours before we went back to the hospital to check on Jeremy. It was bittersweet. Jeremy was still heavily sedated, but my grandparents were in his room when we walked in, so I got to have a long overdue visit with them.

I wanted to ask them if Jeremy could be a witch, but the words kept getting stuck, and I couldn't quite force them out. Mamaw was obviously distraught, and I didn't want to add to her stress by bringing up mythical supernatural creatures. I even caught her more than once absently staring at me with a strange mixture of apprehension and relief. She was clearly going through a whirlwind of emotions and thoughts over what was happening with her grandson.

The whole thing with Jeremy's blood was bothering me, though. I didn't know what else could cause both me and Lucian to react that way around it. Avery said a witch was born to witches, so that could only mean that his family—my family—were also witches and that just didn't make sense either, because I sure as hell wasn't one. Unless . . .

I quickly cast that thought away. Lucian and Malus had both made comments about my unusual gray eyes and even though I'd entertained the idea that my father could possibly have been a vampire on more than one occasion, until I knew for certain, I couldn't base any conclusions about myself on a working theory. Too many things didn't add up with that, either. Just because I'd never met anyone in his family, and we both shared the same shade of eye color with some notorious vampire family, didn't mean he was a long-lost member of it. And it didn't explain how I could've been partly raised by a vampire and not know it. Or the fact that he died when I was eight. Sure, they never found my parent's bodies, but I knew without a doubt that they wouldn't have abandoned me.

But, if my father *had* been a vampire, could that make me a dud witch? That would explain how I wasn't one, but everyone else was. Ugh, I told myself I wouldn't go down that path of thinking. Nothing was making sense or was what it seemed, and it was so confusing. Besides, how could I have been raised the rest of my life by witches and not get some kind of inkling about what they were? No, if Jeremy was, indeed, a witch, then it had to come from Laura's side.

Regardless of if Jeremy ended up being a werewolf or not, I'd made up my mind to just flat out ask him if he was a witch once he finally woke up. Either he would confirm it, or look at me like I was crazy. Either way, we would be able to narrow down our theories about what was going on. A random werewolf attack, or a targeted one.

I still didn't know how long I was going to have to wait to ask him. The bruising that was just beginning that morning had blossomed and now covered the entirety of his swollen face and the portions of his body that were visible. It was heart wrenching to see him that way. According to the nurses, Jeremy had been awake, but it was only once, and it was very brief.

Aiden and I didn't stay too long at the hospital since Aiden was supposed to be having a family night with his parents and younger sister. After I bid my goodbyes to my grandparents, I dropped Aiden off at his parent's house. His vehicle was back at my apartment, so his mom was going to drive him home after their family night.

Lucian and Avery went back to *Silver Moon* when we returned from Glendale. Avery was going to make phone calls to the other packs in the state, and Lucian was determined to begin catching up with his Consul responsibilities. He had a mountain of meeting requests that he needed to see to, and since it was Sunday and the club was closed, he was going to try to get through as many of them as he possibly could.

I was able to control myself both times I'd visited the hospital, so Lucian was trusting me to be alone for a few hours. I'd been looking forward to it, but I was so tired now that it just didn't have the same appeal as before. I grudgingly got out of my Jeep and went up to my apartment. As soon as I was safely inside, I removed my sunglasses and placed them on the kitchen counter. It was six o'clock now, and I hadn't had any blood since that morning. My throat was burning, keeping me well aware of how many hours it'd been.

I opened the fridge and moved all of Aiden's miscellaneous food and drinks to the side, so I could reach the bags of blood in the back. My gums ached in anticipation as I removed two of them, emptied them into separate glasses, and placed one in the microwave. I let my teeth slide down, sighing in relief as the pressure in my gums released.

Once the first glass was slightly warm, I took it out and placed the other in the microwave. By the time it was ready I'd already downed the first glass. Usually I took my time drinking blood to savor the taste, sipping it like a sweet wine, but since it'd been so long since my last one, I couldn't resist chugging it. I rinsed out the first glass before picking up the second one and heading for the bathroom. With the initial hunger out of the way, I could enjoy this one like I wanted while taking a hot bubble bath.

While the tub was filling up, I got undressed and played my favorite music app on low for some soothing background noise. I lit two candles and turned out the lights. The candlelight was so relaxing to my nocturnal eyes, and after spending so much time in the daylight earlier, it was just what I needed.

I placed my glass on the edge of the Jacuzzi tub and carefully climbed in, letting the warmth of the water pull me in deeper until I was in up to my neck. The bubbles floated all around me with their calming lavender fragrance.

I relaxed there for a few minutes before grabbing my glass and finishing it. I set it to the side, slid back down into the water, and closed my eyes. My tingling radar began traveling up and down my skin and I smiled. Lucian was there. I had given him his own key and finally broken him from the habit of knocking first. He was trying to be sneaky, though. I strained, but couldn't even hear him walking through the apartment. The only thing that gave him away was my gift.

"Hello, Lucian," I said as I opened my eyes and saw him leaning against the doorway with his arms crossed.

"Sorry if I'm interrupting anything," he playfully said with a smile. His slight British accent was more pronounced tonight.

"Nope. You want to join me?"

He grinned even wider as he took me in, my nakedness hidden amidst a sea of bubbles. Lucian immediately began to remove his t-shirt and unbutton his jeans. I watched silently as all his clothes came off, one by one, and he carefully climbed in the tub. I repositioned myself to make room for him as he sat down to face me.

The candlelight flickered, casting theatrical light and shadows, highlighting his already impeccable features and seeming to make his emerald eyes blaze with heat. My breath still caught in my throat in moments like this when I looked at him. He was the most gorgeous man I'd ever seen in my life, and my body immediately responded to that attraction, tightening in low places.

"You are so beautiful," Lucian murmured softly. He gazed at me with the same admiration and pure want as I did him.

I smiled bashfully, "I can say the same for you."

I slowly left my sitting position and went to him, careful to float in the water, barely grazing my body with his, and placed a chaste kiss on his lips. Lucian wrapped his arms around my waist, and I moved up to straddle him, placing both of my hands on his chest for support.

"I'm serious, Riley, you have no idea how beautiful you are. I'm the luckiest man on this Earth to have you."

I blushed. Throughout my life, men had always been attracted to me, but I'd never grown accustomed to it. Every time one of them would tell me I was pretty, I never truly believed it. I always thought it was them just telling me those things to get into my pants. It rarely ever worked.

But after meeting Lucian and him constantly proclaiming how beautiful I was, I was actually starting to believe it. And Aiden and Jimmy insisted that even though I was already attractive as a human, now that I was a vampire, my beauty had intensified. I wasn't sure how true that was, because other than my skin being clearer, I couldn't really tell a difference when I looked in the mirror. I still had the same gray eyes, sun-kissed complexion, full lips, and long dirty-blonde hair.

I leaned in for another kiss. This time, we parted our lips and let our tongues caress each other. He drew me against him tighter, pressing the front of our naked bodies against each other. I pulled back from our kiss as I sat fully down in his lap.

The hardness pressing against me, teased my already wanting body.

Lucian's eyes bled to their enhanced visage, and his fangs extended down as he spoke. "Shall we continue this in the bedroom? Our track record for bathtubs isn't so great."

I smirked. On every occasion that we'd attempted to have sex in a bathtub, either one of us ended up hurt, or something got broken. The last time, we attempted to stand in the tub while in the heat of the moment, and I somehow fell face first onto the toilet. I only just caught myself with my hands before doing any damage to my face. If it wasn't for my faster reflexes, I would've had broken bones and an embarrassing emergency room story. "I think that would be wise," I agreed.

He placed both hands on either side of my butt and hoisted both of us out of the water with little effort. I wrapped my arms around his neck, and entwined one hand in his wavy sandy-brown hair. I waited until he stepped out of the bathtub and onto the rug before kissing him once more, this time deeply and thoroughly.

When we broke from our embrace, both of us had lost control, my eyes were now like his, but instead of green streaks peeking through, I knew mine had gray flecks amidst the silvery luminescent hue. We had only made it to the doorway that separated the bathroom and bedroom. I glanced to the bed to judge how far it was when I felt Lucian's lips on my throat. He parted them, allowing me to feel his teeth scraping across my skin.

The temptation of him tasting me was too much. "Bite me," I said breathily as I grinded down on the hardness still pressed against me. He turned us, slamming me against the wall with a hard thud that somehow managed to turn me on even more. Lucian slid his arms underneath my legs and without hesitation bit down into my neck as he simultaneously slid his throbbing erection into my slick core.

I was more than ready for him, but Lucian was not lacking in that area, and he had to shove himself in with all the roughness I was craving. Pleasure erupted from both points of penetration, and I screamed out in decadent agony. I tried to grind down on him, but my legs were still trapped over his arms, and Lucian used that for leverage, firmly holding my body in place.

He slowly went in and out, teasing my wanton body. His heady scent surrounded me, mixing with the smell of blood, and only managed to drive me crazy. I wanted it rough tonight, and he was being too gentle. "Harder," I cried in frustration.

He pulled back from my neck and regarded me for a moment. He grinned wickedly, trails of blood trickling from his mouth, and drove himself in hard. Lucian kissed me as he began his vigorous assault, and the blood passed down my throat. It was mine, so not as appetizing, but it was blood nonetheless, which only caused everything he was doing to intensify.

We continued to drink each other down at the mouth, while Lucian pounded away in an unrelenting and merciless ferocity, until we climaxed together and fell on the floor in a crumpled, tangled mess. As I laid there, attempting to regain myself, I remembered why, even though rough sex was delightfully amazing, we didn't partake in it too often. It would be a solid five minutes before I'd even be able to move.

Lucian was the first to speak, "Well, that's not why I came here, but that was definitely a bonus."

I laughed as I finally managed to sit up. I hadn't been expecting him, either, but I so wasn't complaining. "So, what's up? Did you come here to check on me?" I asked as I gave him the side-eye and leaned back against the wall.

"No." he mimicked my movements and rested against the wall beside me. "I guess I could've called, but honestly, I needed a break from all my meetings, and I thought, 'what better way to take a break, than to come to see you', so I did."

"Yeah, I bet it's been a long day," I agreed. A normal day for his Consul meetings, where the local vampires could request an audience for everything from needing a vampire-friendly job to disagreements with others, was long and tedious, so I couldn't imagine how awful it was today. Since my Becoming, he'd reduced his hours of availability and even skipped some days altogether.

"You have no idea." He rolled his eyes. I don't think I'd ever seen Lucian do that before, it really must have been a bad day. "But, the reason I'm here is because I think I've made a decision on who to hire as my assistant, and I wanted your opinion."

"Oh?" I raised an eyebrow. Lucian had been neglecting, to an extent, more than just his Consul meeting responsibilities while taking care of me after my Becoming. It was already too much for one person to handle, but now that he was behind, and still wanted to spend time with me, he decided it was time to hire an assistant. This person would help Lucian keep track of appointments and take care of some of the more mundane day-to-day responsibilities. It was a good solution to help Lucian get caught up and then be able to actually have some free time.

I hadn't been a part of the interviews or the candidate selection process, but Lucian had been keeping me up to date.

The last time we'd discussed it, he'd narrowed it down to three candidates.

"I really wanted to hire someone I already knew, but the guy who recently moved here is just so qualified." He paused for me to consider his words. "It would be nice to only have to give minimal training to my assistant. I'm afraid the two final local contenders would require much more hands-on instruction than I'd like to take on at the moment."

I nodded my head. I got it. He wanted someone he could trust, but the vampire from out of state would logistically be the better choice. "Do you think you can trust him?"

Trust was a big factor for any vampire in a leadership role. Vampires were cunning, manipulative, and thrived on drama. I considered myself lucky that I was turned by Lucian and lived in this area. Lucian had a reputation for actually caring about others and didn't play those bullshit vampire games. Apparently, there were a lot of like-minded vamps out there who were tired of the politics and just wanted to live in peace, because the vampire population in Louisville was ever-growing. I'd be surprised if Lucian didn't have to hire even more people soon to help out with the rising needs of the vampire populace.

Lucian contemplated that for a minute. "I think so. I mean, I haven't picked up anything negative or conniving from him during our conversations." Lucian's gift was invaluable at times. At first, I'd been embarrassed just thinking about what he was getting from me, and I tried to censor my inner dialogue as best as I could. But after a while, I stopped caring as much, and his being able to pick up on strong emotions and thoughts was almost like second nature to me now. "So, I don't think he has ill intentions. If anything, he seems genuinely eager to get the position."

"Well," I began, "I guess just go with your gut instinct. If you think he's legit and he'd be the best person for the job, then go for it." I shrugged. "If it starts to seem like it's not going to work out, then you can always fall back on one of the other two candidates."

He smiled and leaned down to kiss my forehead. "Thank you." He pulled back and held my gaze. I could see hesitation in his eyes. He wanted to say more. I knew he wanted to tell me that he loved me, but neither one of us had uttered those words since that night when he saved my life. It's not that we both didn't feel that way about each other, we just didn't say it out loud. And I was fine with that. I knew what my heart felt, and I could feel with every fiber in my body that he felt the same way. He hadn't said as much, but I think his hesitation stemmed from not wanting to push me too far, too fast. And I still hadn't figured out where mine came from.

"Well, it's settled then," Lucian confirmed. "I'll go with Bernard and see how it goes. It'll be nice to alleviate some of the stress I've carried with me for so long."

"Yeah, I don't know how you do it." I admitted. It was exhausting just thinking about all those vampires in the region relying on him to take care of any problems they had, let alone having to deal with it. And trust me, they had a lot of issues that needed resolving. I often joked with Lucian that he was more of a vampire babysitter than anything else.

He stood and held out a hand to help me up. "When is Aiden supposed to be coming back?" he asked, nonchalantly.

Lucian wasn't fooling anyone. I knew where he was going with that loaded question. He needed to leave, but didn't want to leave me alone. I gave him a pointed look. "Probably in a couple of hours."

He suppressed a sheepish grin. "Riley, I know you think I'm being suffocating, but I also know that you would never forgive yourself if you lost control."

I sighed as I walked into the bathroom. "I know. But I really think I'm good now."

He leaned against the doorway and crossed his arms. "You did really well today, so I'll ease up a little."

I turned to face him and almost lost my train of thought. Lucian, in all his naked splendor, was almost too much. Warmth pooled in my core again at the sight. "You promise?"

One corner of his mouth quirked. I was obviously sending him all the naughty thoughts running through my mind. "Yes."

I slid back into my bubble bath, before my body betrayed me and pounced on him for round two. He could only afford a small reprieve from his obligations tonight, and I knew I couldn't be selfish. It was an odd war that was constantly waging in my mind, wanting to maintain our individual lives, but not really wanting to share, either.

He gathered his clothes and put them back on as I closed my eyes and enjoyed the waning warmth the water brought my tired and achy—but in a good way—body. Soft lips touched mine for a chaste promise of things to come later. They pulled away and left a searing trail as they grazed my face until resting near my ear. "I'm going back to the club, so I can make arrangements to contact Bernard and get him started on his duties. I have a feeling I'm going to be busy hunting a werewolf."

I looked over at Lucian and gave him a reassuring smile. "Okay."

Once he left, I sunk back down into the water, determined to enjoy the last remnants of the warmth before I had to get out, because I had a feeling I'd be hunting a werewolf with him.

CHAPTER 5

L ucian and I decided to stop by the hospital before our date. I'd been busy at the office all day, so I hadn't had a chance to check on Jeremy yet. Aiden and I were making progress, and if things went well, we might have everything ready to go by tomorrow night. I still wouldn't re-open the office until next week, but it was a relief to know it would be done and ready for new clients.

I'd been thinking about how to bring up the witch issue to Jeremy almost all day, and I still wasn't sure how to go about it. I'd never really been one to beat around the bush, so I was leaning more toward just bluntly asking.

"Did you hear they think it was a bear?" I shot a quick look at Lucian, as two nurses whispered behind us in the elevator.

"Yeah, they said on the news that a few people saw it yesterday and today," the other one chimed in.

"I can't believe it. I never would have thought we'd see a bear attack here."

The elevator dinged, and the doors opened. I couldn't get out fast enough. It felt awkward and somehow invasive to listen to their conversation about my cousin's attack. Aiden hadn't been joking about the bear sightings; ever since yesterday morning, a string of them had been reported in a thirty-mile radius of my uncle's house.

"Are you okay?" Lucian asked.

I nodded and pushed the button for access to the ICU wing of the hospital. Physically, I was fine. I'd made sure to drink right before we left, so I was able to ignore the many smells assaulting my senses. Emotionally, it was iffy. I was holding my own for now, but we'd see how I did once we got in Jeremy's room. It had been over twenty-four hours since the werewolf bit him, so if he'd caught the virus, we should be able to tell by now. Lucian hadn't spoken to any of the supernaturals working at the hospital, so we were walking in blind.

We were buzzed through, and after a few minutes, found ourselves in front of Jeremy's room. I took a deep breath as Lucian opened the door and motioned for me to enter first. Thankfully, there wasn't anyone else in the room; only my sleeping cousin. I stopped next to his bed and looked him over. I couldn't really tell a difference in his injuries from the day before, so I wasn't sure if they had begun to heal, or if I'd just already seen them at their worst.

Lucian came beside me and leaned over the bed. He took in Jeremy's scent and said, "Riley, why don't you tell me what you think?"

Great. He was going to use this as a training exercise. I got it. I mean, how often would I get a chance to sniff out a newly turned werewolf? It just irritated me a little who the unintended experiment subject was. The fact that I was irritated only irritated me more, and the dull humming began in my chest. I quickly stifled my train of thoughts and tried to relax, fully aware it was the vampire in me getting all offended, and I didn't real feel that way.

I leaned over Jeremy as Lucian had, inhaling a lungful of the aromas in the room. Blood was obviously the most pungent smell I could decipher. I pushed that thought away and focused on the underlying smells. Antiseptic. Latex. Urine. And underneath all that were faint traces of a woodsy, musky fragrance. It was a scent I was very used to, but in stronger and larger quantities—most notably in my own apartment. "He's going to be a werewolf."

"Looks that way," Lucian agreed. "I'll make sure I call Avery and let him know. He'll want to pass that along to his Alpha, assuming he hasn't already been informed by someone on the staff here. Your cousin lives in a different pack's territory, but while he's here, he's in their jurisdiction and ultimately their responsibility."

I squeezed Jeremy's hand. Regardless of whether or not he was a witch, there was no denying he was a supernatural creature now. "So, how are they going to break the news to him? Or even to his family? I'm sure everyone's going to notice how fast he's about to start healing."

"I don't know," Lucian admitted. "Vampires and werewolves aren't usually privy to each other's way of handling things. In fact, we usually don't mix very often at all." After a pointed look from me, he added, "The club is an exception. I thought it would be good for our two species to work together, so we could prevent any clashes in this region. It took some time to convince the Alpha to give it a try and it wasn't easy in the beginning, but after many years of trial and error, it runs smoothly now."

I'd have to ask Aiden, then, how they would handle this situation. Aiden's pack had welcomed Amy into their fold, and she started dating one of the security guards at *Silver Moon,* so I'd had a few conversations with her during my stay there. Originally, she'd been nervous about the shift, but after her first full moon, that's all she talked about and was glad she'd been bitten. I hoped Jeremy would feel the same way.

Her situation was a little different from Jeremy's since it was only one bite and easily hidden from her family, but I still wish I would've asked more questions about how the integration into the pack worked. And how, or if, they explained what happened to her family. Vampires didn't allow the newly turned to expose themselves or our species to their loved ones, and I had no idea if werewolves operated the same way.

Lucian's phone buzzed in his pocket. He pulled it out and gave me an apologetic look. "I'll be right back, I have to take this."

I nodded and focused on Jeremy as Lucian stepped out into the hall. It was a such a relief to know he was going to be okay, but I hated this for him. At least I'd been given the option of either dying or being turned into a supernatural creature. Jeremy wasn't given a choice in the matter. How he would react to the news, was anyone's guess. He'd always been more of an optimistic person, so I was hopeful that he would be accepting of his new non-human status, or if he was already non-human, the switch from one species to another.

There was also the uncertainty of how he would react to what I was now. Obviously, I wouldn't be able to keep it a secret from him. Maybe it would be better to deliver one blow at a time? I could let whoever was in charge of filling him in on the supernatural do their job, let him process that for a few days, and then surprise him with the rest. But we really couldn't afford to wait that long to ask him if he had any ties to witches, so maybe it would be better to approach the situation like ripping off a Band-Aid? We could throw everything at him at once, so there wouldn't be any more bombshells for him, and we'd get the information we needed.

"Riley, I'm so sorry, but we have to make a pit stop before the movies." Lucian interrupted my internal dilemma. He stood in the doorway with remorse on his face.

"Is everything okay?"

"Probably." He sauntered farther in the room. "My new assistant, Bernard, received a call about a welfare check on someone. They haven't seen him in a week, and he's not answering his phone. As far as they knew, he wasn't supposed to be going anywhere, so they wanted someone to check on him."

I couldn't stop my eyebrow from arching. "So, you also make house calls?"

Lucian grunted. "Not usually, no."

"Then why do you have to?" I let go of Jeremy's hand and crossed my arms. "Why can't they check on this guy?"

"Because I'm in charge of this area, and they're afraid something happened to him." He gave an exasperated sigh. "If they're right, then it's my responsibility to find out what happened and why. All the vampires know it's my job, so when things like this happen, they automatically call me."

I saw something in Lucian's eyes that I'd never seen before: fatigue and vulnerability. His responsibilities were wearing him down, and he clearly didn't want to admit defeat. Guilt clawed at my gut. I was partly to blame for that look. If he hadn't been so concerned about personally helping me through my Becoming and afterwards, then he wouldn't be so far behind.

"I disagree with that thought." He came closer and took my hands in his, uncrossing my arms. "I already had too much on my plate before you came along. Most Consuls have a team at their disposal to take care of all the things that I do personally— mainly because they don't give a shit about the people they're supposed to be looking after. I didn't want to be viewed the same way, so I thought if I did everything myself, things would be different here."

Lucian gently grabbed my chin, tilting my head up. He placed a soft kiss on my lips and said, "Besides, I'm your Sire, so it was also my responsibility to watch over and guide you. There's no way I'd pass that off to anyone else."

"I think," I began hesitantly, "that you can have a team to help take a lot of the burden off of you and still be the awesome Consul that everyone knows you to be."

He tilted his head, "I'll take that into consideration."

Good. Hopefully, he was being sincere and would actually think about it. "So, where does this guy live?"

"In Old Louisville."

That was only about a ten-minute drive from the hospital. If we left now, we could check on the guy and still have time for our date. Maybe our night wasn't ruined just yet. I nodded my head, "Okay. We'll leave now, so we'll have time to swing by there before the movies."

Lucian pulled me in for another quick kiss. "It shouldn't take long. I really don't think there's much to this. Every time it's happened before, the person just wanted to be left alone for a while, so they were avoiding their friends."

I laughed. Having been avoiding my own friend recently, I could sympathize with that. I withdrew from Lucian and reached down to give Jeremy's hand one more gentle squeeze before we left for Old Louisville.

∞ ∞ ∞

Being a history buff, Old Louisville was one of my favorite places to drive through. It was an almost forty-eight block district that boasted one of the largest collections of restored Victorian homes in the country. Old gas street lamps lined the roads, and you could find everything from Victorian Gothic and Renaissance Revival to Queen Ann and Chateauesque. There were even Tudor-style homes and converted carriage houses nestled in between all the architectural grandeur.

We pulled up in front of the address Lucian had been given, and I stared in awe at the guy's house. I wasn't an expert on architecture, but I had taken an art history class in college, and I knew this particular house, with all the arched windows and doorways on the porch, fell in a Romanesque category. It was three stories of arches, stone, and turrets. And I may or may not have had serious house envy at that moment.

I slammed the car door shut and walked onto the sidewalk. It was dusk, and every house on the street had at least one light on inside, except this one. It was completely dark. Either he had some really good blackout curtains, or he wasn't home.

Lucian knocked several times, rang the doorbell, and knocked again for good measure. We didn't hear a single sign of movement coming from inside. "So, what do we do now?" I asked. "Do we break in, or try again later?"

"Well, we're already here, so let's try all the doors and windows." The front door was locked, and all the windows on the first floor that we had access to were completely covered and sealed shut. The lots in this particular area weren't very large, and there was only about a five-foot space in between each house. Most of the homes restricted access to those areas and the backyard by fences and gates. This house was no different. If we wanted to get in the backyard, we were going to have to scale the fence or go around back to the alley and try our luck there.

"You're joking, right?" I asked incredulously as I sized up the eight-foot wrought-iron fence looming before me. I thought the obvious choice was to take our chances with the alley, not climbing something almost three feet taller than me, and with the exception of one horizontal bar running lengthwise at twelve inches from the ground, nothing to use as leverage to get over it. Not to mention the fact that all along the top were metal Fleur De Lis spikes, ready to impale anyone who tried. But Lucian had walked immediately over to it, like it was the obvious choice.

His only reply was a smirk before he used the horizontal bar as leverage to hoist himself up, grabbed the bottom of one of the spikes, and gracefully vaulted over the damn thing, easily clearing all the pointed Fleur De Lises. He landed quietly on the other side in a crouch . . . still smirking. And the whole show only took a matter of seconds.

"Seriously?" I glanced around swiftly to make sure no one had seen him before giving him narrowed eyes. Did he really expect me do that shit? Obviously, I knew vampires were stronger and more agile than humans, but no one had shown me the extent of what we were capable of yet. I had no idea we could do what he just did.

"It's easy," he claimed, as he straightened back up.

I grunted and crossed my arms. "Yeah, I'm sure it is for someone who's had years of practice."

"Just try it. I promise, you can do it"

Oh, I was sure I could, just not on the first, or tenth try. And the fact that he was still smirking, only secured that thought. "And what if I land on one of those spikes?"

"I highly doubt that." He came closer. "Look, just put your foot here," he pointed in the general area where he'd placed his own, "and push up. Then just grab anywhere at the top of the fence and use your strength to propel your body over." Lucian took a step back. "It's simple."

I really didn't want to do this. I knew I was either going to get hurt, or embarrass myself. Probably both. But I really wanted to go on our date, and the longer it took me to do this, the possibility of having to cancel our plans went up. I was going to have to suck it up and try to be a vampire.

"Ugh, okay." I threw my hands up in defeat. I surveyed the area again to make sure no one was watching us and walked timidly up to the fence. I followed Lucian's instructions, but I guess I didn't put enough oomph into my jump because I wasn't able to grab the top of the fence and slid back down the bars.

I raised my hand to stop Lucian from commenting. There was an amused twinkle in his eye, and I really didn't want to hear his commentary at the moment. I took a deep breath and tried again. My eyes bled to their vampire sharpness, and it seemed like time slowed down as I moved. This time, when I pushed up on the bar, it felt right. I knew exactly how much energy to use and where to place my hands to propel myself up and over the fence, easily clearing the spikes like Lucian had. But my triumphant grin was short-lived. I didn't judge my landing good enough and ended up half landing and half rolling until I came to a stop on my back.

Lucian loomed over me, trying to hold in his laughter. "See, that wasn't so bad. I knew you could do it."

I tried to put my best *fuck you* expression on my face, but it only lasted seconds. I burst into a fit of giggles, because let's face it, if the roles were reversed, I'd have been rolling with laughter at Lucian landing like that. "I think I might need more practice."

He chuckled. "Maybe just a little." Lucian helped me up and wrapped me in a hug. "On a serious note, you did do really well. I'm proud of you." I leaned back and looked up at him. "You never cease to amaze me at how well you're adjusting to all this."

I kissed him. Nothing panty-melting, but a slow and sensual kiss, nonetheless. "Mmm, maybe we should just try again later. I can think of a few more things I'd rather do to you right now." He murmured against my lips.

Heat pooled in my core. Would there ever be a time where a simple look or suggestion from Lucian wouldn't turn me on? I seriously hoped not. Pulling back, I asked, "But what about our date to the movies?"

A wicked gleam filled his eyes. "Oh, trust me, we could do both."

That was tempting. Almost too tempting. I sighed with longing. I knew we needed to do the right thing and see this through. Besides, there would be plenty of time later for whatever he had planned. I could be patient.

"I agree." Lucian gave me another chaste kiss. "As much as I'd like to forget everything except us, we need to take care of this first. Come on," He took my hand, leading me toward the back of the house. "Let's get this over with, so we can begin our night."

We tried the windows first, but they were covered and locked, just like the ones in the front. So, I was shocked when the back door opened right up. "That doesn't seem right," Lucian echoed my thoughts exactly. Why would the guy seal everything else up tight, but leave the back door unlocked?

Once we walked through the laundry area and opened the door to the kitchen, the smell hit us. It was blood. Old blood. Blood that had been spilled several days ago. My eyes turned, and I couldn't stop my fangs from punching down. Everything screamed that something wasn't right, and my body was preparing for whatever laid ahead of us in the house.

"Stay behind me," Lucian whispered. I nodded my accession. I didn't want anything to happen to him, but he was obviously better prepared to deal with any threats than I was. Honestly, I was probably more of a liability than anything else. And I really needed to try to rectify that. If Lucian didn't have time to start training me on how to use my abilities, then I'd see if someone else did.

We crept through the house as silently as possible. I stayed alert. The last thing I needed was something, or someone, sneaking up on us. "Fuck," Lucian swore as he rounded the corner into the front parlor and stopped short.

I cautiously peaked around him. Slumped over on the couch was a headless body. Bile rose in my throat, and I struggled to swallow it. I would not throw up. I was a vampire dammit, a little gore shouldn't make me queasy.

We vigilantly went farther in the room, careful to still keep an eye on our surroundings. There was blood on the man's clothes and the couch, but not as much as I would have expected. I mean, I'd never seen a decapitated body before, but I thought blood would've been everywhere. "Shouldn't there be more blood?" I whispered to Lucian.

He squatted next to the couch and surveyed the area. "Yes, there should be."

I stayed back, not wanting to contaminate any evidence. Besides, I had no idea what to look for, and not knowing how death investigations worked in the vampire world, I was afraid I would only mess things up. Lucian took his time. He examined the body as best he could with minimal contact and walked the entire area, taking everything in.

"Well," he began once he was finished, "I don't think whoever did this is still here. There aren't any decipherable scents that we've come across, and the body has been here for at least four days. It will have to be examined further, but it looks like he was drained and then beheaded."

"Drained?" I asked. "Like by another vampire?"

"I'm afraid so. It looks like there could be puncture marks on his neck, but it's difficult to tell. And whoever cut his head off, was strong. It's a fairly clean cut."

"But I thought vampires didn't usually feed on other vampires?" That was one of the first things Lucian had taught me; that we couldn't survive on another vampire's blood.

"We can't live off vampire blood. That doesn't mean we can't drink it." He gave me a meaningful look.

I blushed. It'd been a while since I'd had that reaction to something Lucian said. He was right. We couldn't live off our own blood, but that didn't mean we couldn't ingest it. Lucian and I had proved that many times over during the heat of the moment. I cleared my throat. "Point taken."

He ran a frustrated hand through his hair. "I'm going to have to make some phone calls. Try to understand what happened here and why. Figure out who his Sire is. Hell, figure out where his head is, for that matter. I didn't see it anywhere. I don't know if it was taken, or placed somewhere else in the house." Lucian gave me an apologetic expression as he pulled out his phone.

I knew that look. That was the look that meant our date night was officially cancelled. I should've known the idea of a night out together was too good to be true. "It's okay, Lucian." I smiled reassuringly. That last thing I wanted was for him to feel like shit for doing his job and solving a murder.

I left him to do his thing and went back into the kitchen, sitting down in one of the chairs at the island. What the fuck was going on? First a werewolf attack that could possibly involve witches, and now a vampire was murdered. If things kept up like this, Lucian wasn't going to have a choice; he was going to need to hire a whole team of people to help him manage and take care of things. Pulling my own cell phone out, I sighed and settled in for a long night.

CHAPTER 6

Bernard, or Bernie, as he kept telling everyone to call him, was about my height at five-foot-five, with light-brown curls hugging his head, hazel eyes, and a thick mustache that looked creepy. Well, it looked that way to me, anyway. Or maybe it was the way he kept staring at me since Lucian introduced us that was creepy. I think it was a combination of both. Either way, he was throwing some major creep vibes my way, and it was making me more than a little uncomfortable.

After Bernie, Avery, and Ellie were finished investigating and taking pictures of the scene, we reconvened back at *Silver Moon*. Lucian explained on the way there that they would try to figure out what happened, but it was the next of kin's responsibility to dispose of the body and settle the person's estate. For a Made vampire that usually meant it was up to the Sire to handle things. If there wasn't a living Sire, or the Sire couldn't be located, then they tried to find a close friend. If all else failed and no one wanted to deal with it, then it fell back on the Consul to take care of. Vampire deaths didn't happen often, so luckily, this was something that rarely had to be dealt with.

And it just went to show that I still had so much to learn about my new world. Being used to the human system of wills, funeral homes, estate lawyers, and autopsies on murder victims, this was a huge adjustment. It didn't seem right to just leave the body there until his Sire claimed it. The human part of me wanted to call the police or even a funeral home to come pick up the body, but I kept reminding myself that these things had to be handled under the human radar. And who was I to come in and try to change the way they've run things for hundreds of years?

"Lucian, Jeffrey is here," Avery announced as he stepped aside so a tall, lanky vampire could enter Lucian's office. He had shaggy blond hair and wore thick black glasses that I knew he didn't actually need.

"Ah, Jeffrey." Lucian shook his hand. "Thank you so much for coming at such a short notice."

Jeffrey bowed his head slightly. "It's no problem, sir. Anything to help my Consul."

Lucian grabbed the laptop and cell phone they'd confiscated from the house. Jeffrey was a software technician and had a reputation for doing a little bit of hacking on the side. Lucian handed both items to him. "I'm hoping you'll be able to get full access to both of these. I need at least the last two weeks of activity on both, but I'd really like a full month if you can manage it."

"Absolutely, sir. Depending on how much security he has, it may take me a few days. But I promise this will be my top priority. I'll get started on it as soon as I get home."

"Thank you, I appreciate it." Lucian and Jeffrey spoke a few minutes more, before Lucian and Avery walked him out, but I tuned them out because Bernie was staring at me again. He was seated across the room with a direct view, so I turned in my own seat to escape his gawking gaze. I was going to have to talk to Lucian about this. It was seriously starting to unnerve me.

I tried to brush if off and focus on what they'd discovered. Thomas—I'd learned was our dead guy's name—did, indeed, have puncture marks on his neck. Multiple marks, to be exact. But it was difficult to tell exactly how many since whoever decapitated him had cut through most of them. The head was nowhere to be found, so the person, or persons, responsible had presumably taken it with them.

I shuddered at that thought. Who would be sick enough to do that and take the head with them? Were they keeping it as a trophy? I couldn't fathom what would make someone do something like that.

"You should take a picture, it lasts longer." Ellie's unmistakable voice cut through my thoughts. She sauntered over and sat in the chair next to me, staring down Bernie in the process.

His cheeks reddened, and he shifted uneasily in his chair. "Uh, sorry. I, uh, was just thinking and was staring off into space. I, uh, didn't realize I was looking at—"

"Yeah, yeah," she interrupted him and waved her hand in dismal, "save it for someone who cares. Don't you have something you're supposed to be doing? Like trying to track down his Sire?" Ellie asked pointedly.

Bernie shot up out of his chair. "You're right. I'll go get right on that." He scurried out of the room without looking at either of us.

Ellie leaned closer toward me, "You know, that guy really creeps me out."

"Thank you! I've been thinking the same thing since I met him earlier. I was wondering if it was just me since Lucian hadn't picked up anything bad or weird from him."

She shook her head, those gorgeous dark-brown curls swishing down her back as she did. "I noticed it right away. I'll be keeping a close eye on him. If he slips up, I'll be the first to know."

"Good. I'm so glad you've got Lucian's back." And I genuinely was. Ellie was fiercely loyal to Lucian. I didn't know much, or really anything, about her past, but I did know that she would do everything in her power to protect Lucian. I counted myself lucky that I could also call her a friend. She was the only vampire, besides Lucian, to reach out and offer advice and help when I found myself neck deep in this world I hadn't known existed.

"No need to thank me. I could never pay him back for everything he's done for me." She trailed off. "But anyway, hopefully, Jeffrey will find some juicy info on that phone."

"'Juicy?'" I asked with a short laugh.

"Yes, 'juicy.'" Her eyes widened in excitement. "I'm betting it was some kind of love triangle gone wrong. And that he got off on getting off while hemorrhaging. That would totally explain everything."

I had to process that for a minute. I didn't know how any of that explained everything, but I settled on inquiring about the most confusing thing she said first. "'He got off on getting off while hemorrhaging?'"

"Haven't you heard about that?" After an unsure shake of my head, she elaborated. "Okay, so you know how some people get off on being strangled or from pain? It's kind of the same thing. When a vampire experiences extreme blood loss, or as we call it hemorrhaging, it won't kill us, but it does make us weak and kind of loopy. Some vampires get extra stimulation while getting stimulated when they're hemorrhaging." She wiggled her eyebrows. "If ya know what I mean."

"Okay," I said slowly. "So, how does that explain everything?"

She rolled her eyes. "Think about it. He had multiple bite marks, and there wasn't much blood, so obviously, multiple people were drinking from him. Why would anyone let that happen unless it was for a hemorrhage orgasm? And since those bites weren't healed, he obviously had his head cut off right after they drank him down. He still had his clothes on, so we know that he, at least, didn't get to do the dirty. That's why I think something went wrong, and he ended up dead."

There was so much that did and didn't make sense about her theory that it was scary. And I didn't know what was scarier, the fact that it could have gone down like that, or that there could be another reason how and why this happened.

"Then explain how someone just happened to have a knife or a sword sharp enough to cut someone's head clean off handy during this orgy?" Avery demanded as he strolled back into the room.

Ellie examined her nails. "Well, I haven't gotten that far yet."

"Yeah, that's what I thought." He stopped next to Lucian's desk and crossed his arms.

She glared at him. "At least I have a solid theory. That's more than you have at this point."

Avery started to reply, but Lucian came in. "That's enough you two." He sank down in his chair and leaned back with his eyes closed.

I stifled a grin. It was nice to know that someone got on Avery's nerves worse than I did. He and Ellie were always butting heads, and I had to admit it was kind of entertaining. Ellie knew all of Avery's buttons to push, and she did it often, mostly for her own personal amusement.

"So," Lucian began, "do any of you think it's a coincidence that we have a werewolf attack and a dead vampire all within the same week?"

"You think it's related?" Avery asked skeptically?

"I have no idea, that's why I'm asking everyone's opinion. Right now, I'm completely clueless on what the fuck is going on in my region."

It hadn't occurred to me the two incidents were related. From everything I'd been told, vampires and werewolves didn't normally work together, Lucian and the local Alpha being a rare exception.

Ellie shifted in her seat. "What would that gain? For a werewolf to attack someone in Glendale and then vampires to feed on and behead another one in Louisville? And how on earth would that be related? You know how well our two species get along."

"Lucian, I think I have to agree with Ellie." Avery looked pained to admit that. "The wolf that attacked Riley's cousin wasn't one of ours and presumably a rogue. It's far-fetched enough to think one would work with a witch, but I definitely can't see a rogue willingly working with vampires. And even if by some miracle that was the case, what's the point of attacking a human two counties away and killing a vampire here? Jeremy and Thomas clearly aren't acquaintances, so what's the connection?"

"Honestly, I have no idea." Lucian acknowledged. "I'm just trying to make sure we look at every angle. And it just seems odd for both incidents to occur so close together."

He had a point. But Ellie and Avery did as well. I didn't know enough about supernatural politics to be able to have a valid opinion. And there wasn't much I could do as a newbie vamp in general, but if there was one thing I was good at, it was getting to the bottom of things. I'd made a career out of it. "I have another week until the opening, so why don't I speak with Thomas' friends? I could dig around and see what I can find out. I can also speak with Jeremy, when he wakes up, to make sure he didn't know Thomas."

Lucian brightened with the idea. "That would be greatly appreciated. Are you sure you don't mind?"

"Of course I don't mind. I don't want to see anyone else get hurt, so I'll do anything I can to help." And I had a feeling we were going to need all the help we could get.

CHAPTER 7

The bruising on Jeremy's face was noticeably less, and the smell of blood wasn't as potent, but the hint of werewolf was slightly stronger than it had been the day before. And he was still fast asleep. The nurses assured me that he'd been awake several times throughout the night, but they'd just dosed him with more pain medicine not long before Aiden and I had gotten there.

"Shouldn't his body be burning through the medicine?" I asked Aiden, once the nurse left. Her scent confirmed that she was also a werewolf, but I didn't feel comfortable asking those kind of questions in front of people I didn't know. She was obviously a member of Aiden's pack, and since I didn't know if he was supposed to be answering questions about his kind to a nosey vampire, I didn't want to take the chance of getting him into trouble.

He waited until we were both seated next to Jeremy's bed before answering. "Not necessarily. You have to remember, the werewolf virus just took hold yesterday, and it won't be the full-fledged thing until after his first shift. Until then, he'll heal faster than a human, but not as quickly as I would. And his body is too busy using all his energy to heal the wounds, so the medicine is still affecting him like a human."

"Huh, I guess that makes sense."

Aiden suddenly became rigid. "Shit."

"What?" I asked alarmed. All my senses went on alert.

"The full moon is Sunday."

With everything going on, I had completely forgotten that a full moon was coming up. "Since he was just bitten, will he still turn so soon?"

"Not usually. The virus would need longer than a week for the pull of the moon to initiate his first shift, but this isn't just any normal full moon." He rubbed his hands up and down his face in frustration. "It's a blood moon."

Like usual, I felt like I should know the importance of what Aiden said, but I didn't. "What's so special about a blood moon?" I really needed to start a list of things I needed to learn about. Moon phases, apparently, needed to go on that list.

"Scientifically speaking? It's a total lunar eclipse, and it makes the moon look red instead of white. Hence, the term blood moon. Supernaturally speaking? It's an extremely powerful full moon and affects all supernatural creatures. Why? I have no fucking idea. But it does. I don't know exactly how it affects everyone else, but for shifters, it makes us less in control and more powerful. If we can't change with the pack in a secluded area, we make sure we're locked up."

Why hadn't I heard about this? Especially since he said if affects all supernaturals? What the hell was going to happen to me on Sunday? "Oh no." Realization dawned on me. "I invited Hattie over for lunch on Sunday."

"As long as she only stays for a couple of hours, it should be fine. But I don't know how long I'll be able to be there. Shifters can feel the impending blood moon a few days before it even happens. And we'll be on edge and hyped up the entire day leading up to it."

"Ugh." I leaned my back in aggravation. Why did I have to be so clueless about everything?

"Just talk to Lucian about it. I'm sure everything will be fine," he assured me. "The bigger problem is Jeremy."

My head snapped in Aiden's direction. "What do you mean?"

"If this were a normal full moon, Jeremy wouldn't feel the pull to change so soon. But since it's a blood moon, there's no question. Riley, he'll shift for the first time this Sunday night."

I looked at my cousin. I thought he'd have more time to come to terms with what he was now. It was already Tuesday, so the poor guy only had five more days until his life as he knew it was over. "How's that going to work? With him being in the hospital?"

"I'm sure the Alpha's already spoken to the shifter staff here and made a plan. Honestly, we don't get many bitten in our territory, so I don't know exactly how it's handled. But, I trust my Alpha, and I know he won't let anything happen to your cousin." He reached over and squeezed my hand for added reassurance.

It was hard to put my faith in someone I'd never even met, but I trusted Aiden, and if he said everything would be okay, and the Alpha would take care of Jeremy, then I had to believe that was going to be the case.

"Breaking news." The television caught my attention. "Angela Jones is live at the scene of the second bear attack this week. Angela, what can you tell us about the developing situation in Shepherdsville?"

Aiden and I shared a look. Shepherdsville was in between E-Town and Louisville. "Thank you, Jim. I'm here in Shepherdsville at the site of the second bear attack this week in our area. The first one was only two days ago in Glendale. As with the first attack, there were no witnesses, but several people have already come forward claiming they saw the bear near the scene afterwards. And while we don't know the identity of the victim yet, police have just confirmed that they did not survive the attack."

What. The. Fuck? I picked up my phone and dialed Lucian's number.

"Riley, how's your visit going?"

"He's still asleep, but that's not why I'm calling. Have you seen the news?"

I could hear a shuffling noise and multiple voices in the background. "No, I've been busy."

"There was another attack. This time in Shepherdsville, and the victim is dead."

"Great. As if things couldn't get any more complicated at the moment."

"I know," I agreed. "This has been a crazy week. Two werewolf attacks and a dead vampire. Lucian, what the heck is going on around here?"

"That's not all."

"What do you mean?" I asked.

Aiden motioned for me to switch the call to speaker phone. As soon as I adjusted it, Lucian's voice rang through the room. "I got another welfare check request this morning for a vampire who lives in the PRP neighborhood. I knew you were going to visit your cousin, and I didn't want to interrupt your plans, so I had Ellie and the other bartender, Alex, go with me to check it out." Aiden and I shared another look. This didn't sound good. "We found essentially the same thing. The vampire was drained and missing his head."

"How long has the body been there?" Even though Aiden hadn't been involved with the investigation the night before, I'd filled him in after Lucian dropped me off at the apartment during the early hours this morning.

One of my favorite things about being a vampire was the fact that I only needed a few hours of sleep each day, and if needed, I could skip a day entirely. It was amazing what you could accomplish when you didn't need as much sleep. I'd even had enough time this morning to get all my meetings setup with Thomas' friends. Aiden and I were going to make our rounds with them later today.

"Thankfully not as long as Thomas. There are still remnants of people's scents in the house, and so far, we've been able to discern four distinct ones, but I only recognize one of them. And that belongs to our dead resident."

That definitely wasn't good. There were a lot of vampires in his region, so I could understand if Lucian just couldn't distinguish who the scents belonged to, but to not even recognize them meant they were here without Lucian's knowledge or consent. When a vampire crossed into a new region, they were supposed to do a check-in with the local

Consul and state their business—whether they were just passing through, staying for a short time, or moving permanently to the area.

"Do you have any wolves there to help?" I knew why Aiden was asking. Even though vampires had a heightened sense of smell, and we could differentiate individual scents, it wasn't anything in comparison to a werewolf's capability.

"No. It's Avery's day off, so he's busy handling pack business. And it's still early, so none of the security team were at the club yet when we left to come here."

"If it's okay with Riley, we'll come down there. I'll sniff around and see if I recognize anyone." He raised his eyebrow at me, silently asking if I had any objections to that plan.

"That's fine with me."

Lucian sighed in relief. "Thank you, Aiden. Riley, are you sure you're okay with that?"

"I already told you I'll help in any way I can." I glanced at Jeremy's sleeping form. "And Jeremy's still heavily medicated, so there's no point in just camping out here while he's asleep. We might as well make ourselves useful."

Lucian relayed the address, and Aiden and I headed over there. The Pleasure Ridge Park, or PRP for short, community was vastly different from Old Louisville. It encompassed a much larger area than Old Louisville, but the homes were nowhere near as extravagant. There were some very nice neighborhoods with houses on the more expensive side in the area, but the home we pulled up to was in need of a lot of repairs and in a run-down section of PRP.

I guess hanging around Lucian for so long, and seeing where Thomas lived, I expected all vampires to have money and live in lavish homes. Come to think of it, I had no idea where any of the others like Ellie actually lived. But I assumed it was in places that would have a little more privacy than this one allowed.

The houses on this particular street were no farther apart than the ones in Old Louisville, but very few had any type of fences to separate them from their neighbors. The house itself, had definitely seen better days. The blue siding was faded and chipped away in several places. Pieces of the gutters were either missing or hanging down, and I couldn't even begin to count how many shingles were missing from the roof.

We went inside, and Aiden made quick work of picking up the scents and tracking three of them back outside, where they disappeared, presumably into a long-gone vehicle. He didn't recognize any of them. I didn't either, but that wasn't saying much. I'd only met a fraction of the vampire population in Louisville.

"He'd only been here for about six months. He was Made in Las Vegas a couple of years ago, but was originally from here, so he wanted to move back. Bernie already contacted his Sire, and she's going to fly in tonight to take care of his remains and belongings." Lucian sounded exhausted as he filled us in after ending his phone call with Bernie.

"How do you know all that already?" I was impressed. They'd only just received the call for a welfare check a few short hours ago.

"Oh, he's got a file on everybody," Ellie answered for him before she sauntered outside.

"That's right," he confirmed. "I have a file on every vampire that legally crosses into my region. It makes things go more smoothly when things like this happen." He must have picked up on my thoughts because he added, "Thomas was an older vampire who'd lived here for over fifty years. Since I don't update my records very often on people while they're here, his Sire information was a little outdated. Bernie's having a harder time tracking him down."

I guess it wasn't unreasonable to assume someone would have changed their phone number or even moved a few times during a fifty-year span. "So, now what?"

He held up a cell phone. "I've got his phone, so I'll drop it off to Jeffrey. I'm hoping there will be something linking our two deceased vampires. I'll take any clue I can get at this point. And we've done as much here as we can, so after I drop this off, I'm going back to the club to take a fresh look at all the facts."

"Don't forget about the second werewolf attack this morning." I reminded him.

"I'm still not convinced they're related, but I'm not going to rule out the possibility. Shifters and vampires usually take care of their own problems, but maybe it's worth a call to the Alpha to see if we can work together on these cases."

Confused, I asked, "I thought we already were?"

Lucian took my hand. "The only reason I was even involved in the attack on Jeremy is because it's your cousin." He let that sink in for a moment. "If it had been anyone else, I wouldn't have gone down there. The wolves would have handled it entirely by themselves."

I looked to Aiden, and he nodded his agreement at Lucian's admittance. For some reason, that seemed wrong to me. Wouldn't things run smoother if they always worked together? Oh well, I filed that away with the rest of my opinions on how the supernatural community should be, but wasn't.

The three of us walked outside, and Lucian locked the front door with the keys he found in the house. Luckily, like Thomas' house, the back door had been unlocked, so they didn't have to actually break in. I wasn't sure if anyone in this neighborhood would've called the police if they saw something like that, but it was always better to be safe than sorry.

My tingling warning erupted before I heard the footsteps coming toward us from the backyard. I tensed, before I remembered Lucian saying Alex had gone with them. He turned the corner and strode over. He and Ellie normally worked the bar together and were very popular with both the male and female clientele. Ellie, with her olive complexion, easy honey eyes that she framed with thick black eyeliner, dark wavy hair that cascaded down her lower back, and full lips that were almost always turned up in a smirk. And Alex with his chiseled features, thick muscular arms, choppy blond hair, and piercing blue eyes. They made quite a team, and I often wondered if there was anything between them, or if they were strictly work friends.

Alex shook his head. "I couldn't find anything in the back yard, besides those three scents. I'm thinking that's how they left."

"I agree." Aiden chimed in. "I think they went in through the front door, but left through the back."

They continued to talk, but my attention zeroed in on one of the street poles. Hiding amongst the cables and underneath an electrical box was a camera pointing down the street. Of course! How had I forgotten that there were cameras spread throughout the city on the electric poles. "Lucian, do you think Jeffrey could hack into the city's camera network?"

Uncertainty filled his face before he looked up at the same pole I'd seen the camera and was swiftly replaced with excitement. "Brilliant idea, Riley. I don't know if he can, but I'll most certainly ask."

Ellie patted me on the back. "Nice catch. The vehicle they left in would have to show up on that camera."

"The body's only been there for about a day, two at the most. So, I'll see if he can pull footage for the last forty-eight hours." Lucian's weariness had been replaced by an animated enthusiasm.

We all left the house after that with a renewed gusto. The cameras could very well be the big break that we needed to figure out who was going around killing vampires in the city.

"Hey, will you stop at this gas station? I want to get a snack." By a snack, I knew Aiden meant about twenty dollar's worth of food. Werewolves had a crazy high metabolism, and it seemed like all he did was eat.

"Sure," I told Aiden. "I need to get gas anyway." I pulled in and parked next to an empty pump. Aiden went in the store to get his snacks, and I got out to fill up the tank. A tingling chill swept through me as I leaned against the Jeep, filling me with an odd and sudden nervousness. It was similar to the usual vampire warning system I'd become used to, but somehow different.

I looked around, trying to find the vampire who triggered my gift, but my eyes were drawn to a group of trees across the highway and beyond the railroad tracks that ran parallel with it. The uneasiness I felt grew stronger the longer I stared in that direction. And an altogether different shiver ran through my body because I knew what was hidden behind those trees. When I was a little girl, and my grandparents would come up to

Louisville to go to the mall, I was always scared when we drove past it. I would squeeze my eyes shut when I saw it peeking above the trees in the distance and wouldn't open them again until I'd counted to at least one hundred.

The trees had grown a lot since then. You couldn't even see it looming there on its hilltop from the highway anymore. But I knew it was there. Now that I was older, things like that didn't usually bother me anymore. It wasn't that I didn't believe in ghosts, but until I had an experience of my own, the jury was still out. For some reason, though, that was the one place that still managed to give me the creeps.

I'd never been inside the building, just seeing it from a distance was always good enough for me, but people came from all over the country to take a tour of the famous Waverly Hills Sanitorium.

"Hey, are you okay?" Aiden pulled me out of my trance.

"Yeah." I frowned as I realized I'd already finished getting gas and had placed the nozzle back on the pump. The tingling uneasiness on my skin had ceased, so whoever had triggered it was now long gone. "Hey, what do you know about Waverly Hills?"

"The old tuberculosis hospital?" He opened the passenger door and set his bag of snacks on the seat." Not much. I know a lot of people died there, and they do ghost tours during the summer, but that's about it. Why?"

"It's nothing," I started to say, but stopped short as a deep growl emanated from Aiden.

"Get in the vehicle, Riley." He snarled as he closed his door and glanced around the gas station.

Stepping toward the front of the Jeep, I scanned the area. "What is it?"

"Get. In. Now." Aiden's voice was dangerously low as he punctuated each word. It wasn't until he pinned me with amber eyes that I slowly backed up and followed his orders. Aiden was always so calm and in control, that I knew it had to be serious for his restraint to be slipping. I even went a step above and beyond and locked the doors when he stalked away from the Jeep, back toward the store.

Aiden was only gone for about ten minutes, but it seemed like a lifetime. I felt bad for hogging a pump for that long, but not knowing what happened for him to be ready to expose his wolf in public like that, had me scared to move.

"We need to go to *Silver Moon*," he demanded as soon as he slid in the vehicle.

There was no way I was going anywhere until he explained what the fuck just happened. "Why? What was that about?"

He regarded me with uncertainty. "Let's just go to the club, and I'll–"

"No." I interrupted. "You don't get to go all wolfy on me, demand that I get in the car, and not give me an explanation for it." My gums throbbed, barely holding back the sharp canines that wanted to announce themselves to whatever threat Aiden had perceived. The now familiar pain in my chest began to hum. I was equal parts scared for the reason behind his actions and pissed that he was trying to put off telling me precisely what that reason was. I knew I was probably overreacting, but I couldn't control these stupid vampire emotions.

"Fine." He huffed and glanced around the gas station anxiously. "But please start driving. We need to hurry up and get there."

My vampire settled down, and the pulsing in my chest quieted. I could work with that compromise. I started the engine and pulled away from the pumps.

Aiden's attention remained focused on our surroundings as I exited the parking lot. "It was him, Riley."

There was only one *him* that he would be referring to. And if that was the case, Aiden's reaction at the gas station made absolute sense. I gripped the steering wheel tight, hoping I was wrong. I knew we'd eventually hear from him again, but I thought I'd have longer to prepare myself. I'd almost died because of him. He'd kidnapped me and had Aiden beaten within inches of his life. And all so he could turn and use me in his plot to expose the vampire race.

Half of his plan for me came true, but not by his hands. His minion, Jessica, stabbed me and Lucian saved my life by turning me into a vampire. He fled, and no one had seen him since that night. I had no idea why he would come back to Louisville, unless it was to finish what he started. But I had news for him, there was no way in hell I would join him—at least willingly.

I cringed at that thought. I still had the occasional nightmare about him. Lucian was concerned it was Malus invading my dreams—which unfortunately was Malus' gift—but having experienced that firsthand on two separate occasions before my kidnapping, I knew the difference. Luckily, it was only flashbacks I'd been having. They were still scary in their own right, but nothing compared to having the real thing take control of your dreams.

"I sensed a vampire while you were in the store," I confessed, almost whispering. "But it was different." I cleared my throat. "I don't know how to explain it, but it was the same sensation I normally get, only laced with . . . I don't know . . . anxiety? Maybe nervousness? It had me on edge, and I was trying to figure out what was going on when you came back out."

"I hate to say this, Riley, but I think it was warning you that the vampire wanted to harm you."

I swallowed hard. As much as I didn't want Aiden to say it, I needed to hear the name. I needed to know exactly who he thought had been there. "Who was it, Aiden?"

"I think you already know."

I stopped at a red light and turned my head toward him. "I want you to say it."

A mix of sympathy and anger filled his eyes. "Malus."

CHAPTER 8

"**A**nd you're certain?" Lucian asked for the third time.

Aiden was unwavering. "I would know that scent anywhere. I'm a hundred percent positive it was Malus."

"None of this makes sense." Lucian paced around his office. "I can't rule out the possibility that he could've been at the first house, but I know for a fact he wasn't at the second house this morning. Like you, I could identify his scent instantly. We spent too much time tracking him during his last stint in Louisville."

"Maybe he's spent the last two months rounding up more followers?" I suggested. Laying low and regrouping to try again sounded exactly like something Malus would do. I just didn't know why he would come back to Louisville for that second try.

"You've got a point," Lucian agreed. "And that only makes me more confident in the decision I made."

Aiden leaned back in his chair. "You called him."

Lucian sighed, nodding. "I didn't see that I had a choice at this point. I've got two murdered vampires and Malus' scent near one of the murder scenes."

I was feeling a little lost. "Um, called who?"

"My sire," Lucian said somberly.

I'd never met him, and Lucian rarely spoke of his Sire, so I didn't know much about the guy. The only things I knew for certain was that he'd turned Lucian into a vampire in the early eighteen hundreds, and he was now the Dominus of one of America's six territories. The one we lived in, to be precise. That's how Lucian came to be the Consul of this region. His Sire asked him to take over the job, and Lucian wouldn't, or couldn't—I still wasn't sure exactly how that went down—tell him no.

"So," I began, "is this a bad thing?" The room suddenly seemed gloomy, giving me the impression things were about to get bad because of Lucian's decision.

"Not necessarily," Lucian replied carefully. "Sebastian is one of the good guys. A little arrogant and conceited at times," he smirked as if he was recalling long-forgotten memories, "but he and I share a lot of the same beliefs when it comes to the vampire and supernatural communities."

"Why do I feel like there's a but?"

"Because there is. He'll have to contact the Low Council about getting a BloodGuard unit sent here. Normally, that wouldn't be too bad, but he'd just put in a request before we found Malus the last time, so this will be the second time this year he's had to petition them for our region. It's going to bring attention here. And having the Council's attention trained on you is something you never want."

The Low Council was also something I didn't know much about. Lucian and the other Consuls reported to their Dominus and those six reported directly to the Low Council. Each country had their own Low Council that governed their vampire population. "Didn't you tell me before that the Low Council was made up of House Heads?"

"Most of the positions are filled by House Heads from some of the vampire Houses in the United States. There are seven members of the Council. Five are also Heads of their own Houses and the other two are unHoused vampires." He leaned back in his chair. "And yes, to answer what you're thinking, they epitomize everything you've heard about the typical House vampire. They're conceited, conniving, and only worried about what benefits them."

And that's why I really didn't care to learn more about vampire politics. How could an entire species be ruled and governed by a group of people who were only looking out for themselves? I'd yet to meet a Housed vampire, so I didn't know firsthand how bad they were, but I'd been told enough stories to have a general idea. And I was more than glad that the closest vampire House was a few hours away and in another region. I wasn't jumping at the bit to meet any of them any time soon.

"So, what did he say?" Aiden leaned forward in his seat.

"Nothing yet. I had to leave a message and I'm waiting for him to call me back."

As if on cue, Lucian's phone rang on his desk. He looked down. "Well, here goes nothing." He picked up his phone and answered.

Aiden rose from his seat and gave me a look that clearly said, we should give Lucian some privacy. The nosey in me didn't want to leave. I wanted to stay and hear first-hand what his Sire had to say. But I relented with a frown and followed Aiden out of Lucian's office.

"I'm going to go find Jimmy. He's supposed to work tonight and should already be here," Aiden said as we walked out of the employee only hallway and into the main dance area of *Silver Moon*.

Jimmy, Aiden's best friend and fellow werewolf, worked at the club like the other members of their pack on the security team. When Aiden had stayed with me before, as extra protection from Malus, Jimmy had become an almost permanent fixture at my apartment. The three of us had spent many nights watching movies, playing games, and me observing in awe at just how much food two werewolves could put away.

I was about to go with Aiden, until I saw Ellie and Alex behind the bar. As much as I wanted to see Jimmy, I knew he was supposed to be coming over in the next few days for our first movie marathon since Aiden moved back in, so I told Aiden I'd catch up with him in a few minutes. Other than during the two vampire death investigations, I hadn't really seen Ellie much since I moved back in my apartment, and I wanted to check in with her.

"Hey," I said to both of them as I sat down at the empty bar. The club wasn't open yet, since it was still the afternoon, but they were busy getting their prep work done before the first wave of weekday partiers came in.

Alex nodded in my direction and continued to wipe out the glasses. "Hey, girlie," Ellie called over her shoulder. She placed the last two bottles of bourbon from her box on the shelf behind the bar and came over to me, leaning against it. "Did you miss me already?"

Ellie could always bring a grin out of me. "I wish that's why we stopped by. After Aiden and I left, we stopped at a gas station, and Aiden caught a whiff of Malus' scent."

Her eyes widened before narrowing. "Are you fucking kidding me?"

"That's exactly how I feel." I agreed. "Now, we just have to figure out why."

"I'll tell you why," she crossed her arms, "because the dude is a fucking psycho."

"I definitely agree with you there."

A familiar seductive laugh echoed down the stairs that let up to the VIP area of the club. It also held the donor rooms where human volunteers allowed vampires to feed from them. Since I refused to drink straight from someone's body, other than Lucian's, I'd never been up there. The idea of being that intimate with some random person made me nauseous. Obviously, most of the other vampires didn't share my squeamish sentiment, hence the private rooms for the practice, so I tried not to judge. Besides, who knew what the future would hold? In thirty or forty years I may be over my qualms about drinking straight from the vein and indulge regularly. I seriously doubted it, but I'd learned long ago to never say never.

Ellie rolled her eyes. "Great," she muttered under her breath. "Just the person I wanted to deal with today."

The clicking of what I knew were knee-high lace-up boots with a ridiculously long heel began their descent down the metal staircase. I kept my gaze averted anywhere but in that general direction in the hopes she wouldn't come over to the bar area.

While I had been living at the club, I'd tried to keep up with her schedule just so I could avoid her, but she seemed to always run into me no matter where I hid out.

"Well, look who we have here," a Spanish accent purred next to me.

I glanced at Ellie, who was unabashedly staring the new arrival down. "If you came over here to start some shit, you might as well just walk away."

"Oh, don't be like that, Ellie." She leaned against the bar next to me and brushed her arm with mine. "I just wanted to say hi." She feigned an innocent, sympathetic look toward me. "And see if Riley was okay during her break from Lucian."

Too bad I knew better. Brianna was anything but innocent or sympathetic to anything that involved me. During the search for Malus, Lucian had to call in reinforcements, and Brianna, unfortunately, was one of the vampires that heeded his plea. She was an old flame of Lucian's and reminded me of that fact every chance she got.

She also hated humans and believed vampires were better than them. I was naïve enough to believe, at first, that she would start treating me better after I made the transition to a vampire, but it only seemed to make things worse. The girl seriously had it out for me. She even went as far as trying to get me to lose control every chance she got.

While I *was* grateful for her help, especially during the fight with Malus, I'd hoped she would leave Louisville and crawl back to wherever she'd been before Lucian asked her for help. But she was still here. And as far as I knew, she didn't have any plans to leave any time soon.

Ellie tried to assure me that Brianna's behavior toward me only stemmed from the fact that she was jealous that Lucian and I were together, and eventually, she would stop being a bitch. I wasn't so sure. Regardless, Ellie had taken on the full-time job of keeping Brianna at bay, and I couldn't love her more for it. But, there was only so much she could do.

"You know perfectly well we're not taking a break, Brianna," I said flatly. Despite wanting to elaborate more, I refrained from clarifying further. I had a bad habit of over explaining myself when it came to my decision about moving back to my apartment and taking our relationship slow. I think sometimes, I tried to talk myself into justifying that it was the right decision to make. Besides, it was simply none of her business, and I knew she was just trying dig for some more information.

She had the audacity to smirk at me. And as much as it irritated me, and I hated to admit it, even smirking she was beautiful. Her perfect olive complexion, hip-length dark hair, full pouty lips, and curvy figure that she always made sure to flaunt. She was a member of the security team, but instead of the standard black t-shirt and jeans, she always chose to wear tight jeggings and the skimpiest halter top she could find to display those curves.

"Hey, Brianna." Alex slid next to Ellie.

Brianna, already leaning against the bar, used her arms to push her cleavage out even further in her black low-cut top. "Oh, hey, Alex." She batted her eyes.

Ellie and I exchanged a look, and I barely contained my eye roll at her antics. It was a well-known fact Brianna wanted Lucian, but since she wasn't getting anywhere with him, she'd been turning her attention toward Alex lately.

"Would you mind doing me a favor?" He gave her the full force of his penetrating blue eyes.

"Of course." She leaned further onto the bar, somehow managing to expose even more cleavage.

Alex glanced down, confirming her efforts weren't going unnoticed. "Could you go to the stock room and get me another case of glasses? I had to help Lucian out earlier, and I'm a little behind." He ran a hand up and down the back of his head and gave her a sheepish grin. "It would help me out so much if you could do that for me."

"Well, I am supposed to be doing my rendezvous with the security team soon, but I think I have time to grab them first."

He sighed in relief. "Thanks. I really appreciate it."

"Oh, you can thank me later." Brianna winked. She gave me and Ellie a parting sneer before turning and sauntering away.

Once she was out of hearing range, we all burst into laughter. "Well, that's one way to handle her." Ellie slapped Alex on the back.

"You both owe me, now," he said, grimacing. "You know I just opened a door that I'm not going to be able to close easily."

Afraid she was already back, I glanced behind me when I heard a door open and close. Luckily, it was only Lucian. He sat down next to me.

"So, how did it go?" The anticipation was killing me.

"Well, needless to say, he wasn't happy with this developing situation. He never officially withdrew the request to have BloodGuard assistance the last time Malus was here, so he's going to contact the Council and see if it can be expedited. Sebastian thinks we can get someone down here possibly by the weekend."

Ellie sucked in a deep breath and seemed a little pale. "This weekend?" she asked hesitantly.

"Yes. And I'm sure I won't know who or how many until they actually show up." Lucian gave her a look that I couldn't quite decipher. Sympathy. Regret. Maybe a mixture of both? "But, and I hate to admit this, I think I need them here to capture him. At the rate he's going, we can't afford for it to take as long as it did the last time."

She nodded, but didn't say anything else. That was odd. I'd never seen Ellie at a loss for words, and she seemed shaken by Lucian's news. This week just kept getting stranger and stranger.

CHAPTER 9

A iden and I spent the rest of the day and night interviewing all of Thomas' friends. The only things we really learned were that Thomas wasn't an overly active socializer, and he had a fondness for riverboat cruises. Those were the only recurring themes during each meeting. The remainder of our time was spent listening to them reminiscing of the good old days and telling us they couldn't believe he was gone.

I felt like we wasted almost an entire day. Especially since my grandmother had called with the news Tuesday night that Jeremy was finally fully awake. By the time we were finished with all the interviews, though, it was too late to visit him. And honestly, that was probably a good thing. As much as I wanted to see him, I was also nervous. I still hadn't figured out how to bring up the whole witch thing. And I was too exhausted after the eventful day we had to even attempt to figure it out.

Several hours of sleep and a blood bag or two later, I was re-energized and reluctantly ready to face the music. Sort of. While

I watched Aiden scarf down his breakfast for two with envy, I tried to go over everything in my head. Two werewolf attacks in two different cities. Two vampire murders right here in Louisville. None of the victims seemed to be connected—that we knew of yet. Throw in a possible witch's potion and the sudden appearance of Malus, and we had a total clusterfuck that just didn't make sense.

If Malus was the orchestrating factor for all of these events, then I'd completely pegged him wrong. The last time he was here, he'd been building an army of followers, so they could go on a killing spree during a live television broadcast. I honestly thought that if he ever did try for round two, he'd skip all the dramatics and go straight for public exposure. Humans weren't going to know about the vampire deaths, and there weren't any witnesses when the werewolf attacked, so I had no idea how they were supposed to help his end game.

No, something wasn't right. There were obviously pieces of this puzzle that we were missing. Important pieces. I just hoped we figured them out before anyone else got hurt.

"You ready?" Aiden asked as he rinsed his plate off in the sink.

I nodded my head and slid off the barstool. Reluctant as I was to know the answers to the questions I needed to ask Jeremy, the sooner we knew, the sooner we'd have another piece or two of that puzzle.

We were barely out of the parking lot when Lucian called and asked if we could make a detour. Jeffrey had a lead from the phones and computer we'd taken from both of the crime scenes, but Lucian couldn't get away for a while. He was in the middle of arranging the weekly blood deliveries for the local vampires.

Since I was one of those people he was busy trying to take care of with those convenient deliveries, I thought it was only fair that we helped him out and swung by there on our way to see Jeremy.

Jeffrey ended up living in a Condo off Main Street not too far from the hospital, so it actually worked out better for us to stop by than Lucian having to drive all the way over there. We easily found a parking spot on the road and went up to his Condo.

"Hey, come on in," he said after he answered the door.

"Thanks. Love the shirt, by the way." He looked down and then looked at me, realizing we both wore the same band t-shirt. That brought out a shy smile, highlighting his dimples. Even though he was a little on the geeky side, like all the other vampires I'd met, he was attractive. I bet he could get any girl he wanted. But I also had a feeling that he'd been a shy introvert before he was Made, and turning into a vampire hadn't really changed that much. Personally, I thought it just made him even more adorable.

"Yeah. Best band of the seventies," he stated matter-of-factly, with more self-assurance as he led us to a desk in the living room.

"Absolutely," I agreed and stared at his setup in awe. There were four monitors spread across the desktop, two towers sitting on the floor, and three external hard drives resting next to them. There was no telling what kind of power that setup had.

He sat down in front the impressive arrangement and sheepishly admitted, "Uh, I don't really have any extra chairs. Unless, you want to bring over a couple of them from the dining table?"

"No, it's fine," Aiden said. "We can stand."

Jeffrey looked unsure, but after a nod from me, shrugged his shoulders and turned back toward the monitors. "So, I won't bore you with all the technical lingo of how I retrieved the information, but it did take quite a bit of hacking to get it."

He opened a few folders and then pulled up the internet on one of the monitors. "Let's begin with the phones and laptop. Both phones had a series of text messages from the same number during the days leading up to the murders."

I glanced at Aiden as Jeffery continued. "I don't want to go into detail," he said with a blush, "but they were very explicit in nature and involved both parties meeting up for a night of pleasure."

Shit. I couldn't believe it. Ellie may have actually been on to something. "In the text exchanges for both of the deceased vamps," he opened some of the files, so we could see screenshots of the text message transactions, "it seemed like the other person got their number through a website or email exchange. So, next I checked their email accounts and recent website activity."

After a few more clicks, we also had visual confirmation of an email where phone numbers were swapped. "Through those, I was able to trace the source of where our two victims met the person who was supposed to go to their house for," he hesitated, "uh, you know." Jeffery cleared his throat. "For a fun night," he finally managed with another blush.

"Are you saying they met someone online for a hookup?" Aiden provided.

"Yes. That's exactly what I'm trying to say." Jeffery sighed in relief. "So, there's this website where you can buy and sell items.

Kind of like a nationwide online classified section. But, just like the classified section in a newspaper, there's also an area where you can meet people. Think of man seeking woman, woman seeking woman, you know that kind of thing."

He pulled up the website and went to the area he was referring to. "Both of our victims responded to the same ad. The person who posted it made a reference to drinking Venae, so it would attract the attention of vampires." Ah, very clever. Venae was the term vampires used to order blood from vampire-owned restaurants, bars, and even inside Lucian's club. "A few hours after they made contact, the victims received an email with a phone number. Through texting, they were asked if the meetup could be at the victim's place. And well, you know what happened after that."

"So, they're picking them up through an internet ad?" Yep, Ellie had to be right.

"Do you have the exact ad?" Aiden asked.

Jeremy scrambled through the papers on his desk. "I have all the information on this flash drive." He handed it over to Aiden. "The link to the ad—which is still up, by the way—the emails, and screen shots of the texts. I tried to trace the phone to an owner, but it was a pre-paid phone you can buy anywhere with no real information on who owns or purchased it. I also tried to track the owner of the ad, but so far I'm not having any luck. That website has some pretty good security."

"Wow, you've thought of everything." I was impressed.

His cheeks reddened again. "Oh, and I was able to hack into the city's camera network and get stills of the vehicle going to the second victim's house and leaving. It's pretty grainy, but you can see at least two individuals in the car. Unfortunately, there wasn't a license plate on the vehicle, so I couldn't track down who the vehicle's registered to."

I raised an eyebrow.

"There aren't any cameras on the first guy's street, but there was one on the corner of a nearby intersection. I pored through all the footage in a three day window and I found, what I think is the same vehicle, driving toward his house and then again driving away from it about two hours later. That was six days ago."

"Good work Jeffery," Aiden praised, with the same surprise and awe in his voice that I felt. This guy was no joke. He could make my life a whole lot easier once I started accepting new cases next week. "Lucian may have more work for you in the future."

Jeffrey beamed with pride. "I'd be more than happy to help my Consul any time he needs it."

"I have to say, I'm a private investigator, and I'm seriously impressed. Would you ever consider doing the occasional side job for me? I'd pay you, of course." I quickly added. I didn't want him to think I was trying to piggyback off Lucian. Or that he needed to feel obligated to do anything for me for free.

He brightened at that proposition. "I'd love to." I started to tell him that he could say no, but he held up a hand. "Really, I love doing this kind of stuff. It's like a challenge for me, and if I can get paid to do it, then that just makes it all the better."

"Great." I smiled. "If a case comes up where I think you could help, I'll reach out and see if you're available and willing to take it on."

"Sounds good to me." He stood and shook hands with both of us. "I'll be looking forward to it."

We relayed the news to Lucian once we were back in the Jeep. Like Aiden and I, he was hopeful the information Jeffrey found would give us our first lead with these murders. As I pulled into traffic and headed to the hospital, it was first time all week that I actually felt a little optimistic. And I couldn't help but wonder how long that feeling would last.

∞ ∞ ∞

"You honestly expect me to believe you had no time to react?" a shrill, whispered voice demanded from Jeremy's cracked door.

I immediately stopped in my tracks and gave Aiden wide eyes. I'd know that voice anywhere. It belonged to Jeremy's mother, Laura.

"I don't care what you believe," Jeremy answered nonchalantly.

"Well, let me tell you what I think." The click of her heels across the floor abruptly stopped. "I think you're acting like you're okay with this."

"It's not like I have a choice, mother," he bit out.

"There's always a choice. You could have easily prevented this."

"Laura, please, that's enough." My uncle sighed. "He's been through enough, as it is."

"*You* shouldn't even be here," she hissed at Unlce Brian. "You should be down there tracking this monster."

"You'd better be careful with the name calling." My cousin snickered.

115

"Oh, is that it? This is funny to you? Do you have any idea what this will do to our reputation?"

I felt guilty. I didn't want to listen in on this very private family conversation, but I couldn't help but hear every word with my enhanced hearing. I motioned to Aiden for us to go ahead and leave. I'd just come back later—preferably when Laura wasn't there.

"Laura," my uncle barked. "Give him a break. He didn't ask for this."

"Give him a break?" Her voice raised, almost becoming perceptive to those without supernatural hearing in the hallway. "Of course you wouldn't care. Your family's reputation was already tarnished enough by your mother and sister," she sneered.

I stopped in my tracks, again. I was willing to walk away from this bizarre conversation up until she mentioned my mom and grandmother. I'd had to endure enough of that woman's petty and snarky comments as a child, but I damned sure wasn't going to let her talk shit about my family now.

I turned on my heels and marched right into the room as if I didn't have a care in the world, and didn't just hear every single word of her cattiness.

Jeremy's head snapped up. He grinned wide, but it faltered for a moment. I walked right past my aunt with my head held high and gave my uncle a quick hug before turning my attention to Jeremy. "Hey, I'm so glad you're finally awake."

"Why don't we go ahead and leave?" my uncle asked Laura with clear relief that the conversation had been interrupted.

"Fine." She narrowed her eyes at Jeremy. "We'll discuss this again later." She shot me and Aiden a look I couldn't quite decipher before she stormed out of the room. My uncle apologized for her behavior—even though she wasn't his responsibility anymore, it was clearly a habit from so many years of being married to her—and followed Laura out of the room, closing the door behind him.

I introduced the two guys to each other, and Aiden and I sat down in the chairs next to his bed. I looked him over and was surprised at how good Jeremy looked. I could see a huge improvement since the last time we'd been there the day before.

"I'm sorry," Jeremy said to Aiden.

Confused, I looked between them. "Sorry for what? You just met."

He looked down sheepishly. "For what my mother said. I know you both heard her."

I raised an eyebrow.

"He knew we were in the hallway for most of that delightful conversation," Aiden offered.

Jeremy nodded and pointed to his ear. "The hearing has already improved. You wouldn't believe what I've been picking up," he joked half-heartedly.

Ah, so someone had already explained what he was. I tried to hide the sympathy from my face, but it must have slipped out.

"It's okay, Riley. Really, I'm okay. Obviously, my mom isn't thrilled . . ." He let that sentence hang.

"I'm surprised they told your parents," Aiden admitted.

"Oh, nobody told them. They figured it out by themselves."

I'm not sure how long the three of us sat in weighted silence after his admission. It was obvious Jeremy and I both had things we wanted or needed to say, but weren't sure where to begin.

Aiden finally broke the silence with a huff. "If Riley's not going to ask, then I will. How were your parents able to figure it out?" He shifted in his seat, so he could look fixedly at Jeremy. "I can only imagine one scenario where you being a werewolf would ruin your family's reputation. And if that's the case, then they would've easily been able to figure out what's happening to you, because that means you already weren't human. Am I right?"

"Aiden!" Granted, those were the same general questions that I had and planned on eventually asking myself, but the execution was too blunt for my taste. For anyone else, yes. But this was Jeremy, and I felt like we needed to ease into this conversation and not dive right in.

"No, it's fine Riley," Jeremy promised. "I was going to have to tell you eventually anyway, especially since you're not exactly human anymore yourself." My mouth flew open. How did he know? "Which, I'm really going to need you to tell me how that happened. And figure out how Mamaw was able to keep that gossip to herself."

What was he talking about? Why would he think our grandmother would be aware of my non-human status?

"Sorry, I know you're confused." He reached for my hand. "I wanted to tell you so many times growing up, but I was forbidden to let you know about our family."

There were no words to describe how I felt in that moment. My heart skipped a beat, and my entire body stilled, preparing for the revelation that I already knew was about to come.

"We're witches, Riley. Well, most of our family. You, dad, and Papaw aren't, but the rest of us are. Or were, in my case," he added remorsefully.

"Shut the fuck up." I stood, my chair screeching against the floor. I'd known this was a possibility, but I'd assumed it was a long-shot. "I don't understand. If I come from a family of witches, then how did I not know growing up? Mamaw and Papaw never went to Coven meetings, or practiced any kind of rituals or spells. I mean, wouldn't I have seen something? Or had some sort of inkling that those things were going on?"

"Ah, I see you've learned about witches. I guess since you joined the other team?"

I didn't want to admit that I'd only just found out about witches that week, so I crossed my arms and said, "I've learned a few things since then. But what I *have* learned doesn't make any sense."

"Well, for starters, Papaw isn't a witch." He sat up in bed, grimacing. "So, when Mamaw insisted on marrying him, she was thrown out of her Coven."

"Witches always stick to their own kind." Aiden agreed. I glared in his direction.

"Exactly. Witches are all about purity and marrying into more powerful families. And since one of their children inherited magic and the other one, my dad, didn't, you can see why. There's no guarantee a child of a human and a witch will have magic, so they avoid those matches all together."

"So, you're saying my mom was a witch, then?"

"Yes."

The pieces were beginning to add up with the conversation we'd just overheard. "So, I take it Laura is a witch?"

"Yep. She only married my father hoping our family's magic would somehow pass through him and to me."

"Why, what's so special about our family?"

"Aside from the fact that we're fire witches and can throw a mean fireball?"

Aiden whistled. I glared at him again. He raised his hands in surrender. "I'm no expert on witches, but I know when one can control an element, in addition to crafting spells, it's a big deal."

Jeremy nodded. "That's right. The ability to harness an element is coveted in the witch community and tends to run in families. But, our family can also sense other supernatural creatures."

Aiden and I both jerked our heads toward Jeremy. "Say what, now?" I couldn't control fire, or cast any spells—that I knew of, it's not like I'd ever really tried—but that particular ability is what spawned the entire chain of events that led to me currently being a vampire.

Aiden actually had the audacity to laugh. "Everything makes so much sense now."

My vampire was getting mad. My whole life was a lie. I came from a family of witches. And the fact that no one thought it was important to tell me that bit of information really pissed me off. Especially since, apparently, I'd inherited at least one of the family witch traits. I doubt knowing about my 'gift' beforehand would've changed much with how the ordeal with Malus went down, but at least I wouldn't have been completely clueless about it.

How could they lie to me my entire life? And if my grandmother could sense supernatural creatures then she had to have known that Lucian was a vampire when I took him down for dinner a couple of months ago. I wonder why she didn't say anything. She acted like she didn't even notice what he was.

Dread set in as I realized she had to already know about me, too. She wasn't staring absently at me the other day because she was worried about Jeremy, it was because that was first time I'd seen her since my turning. That whirlwind of emotions I saw on her face was probably her trying to figure out how she felt about a witch having a vampire granddaughter.

I sat back down in my seat as an unsettling thought crept up. My eyes. I had my father's eyes and Malus and Lucian had made comments about a vampire family having the exact same gray color. As much as I wanted to know more about that, I also didn't want to know, so I'd never pried for more information from Lucian. But I'd be lying if I said I hadn't questioned if my father was a vampire ever since then. I'd held on to the belief that he wasn't since I didn't think a vampire could've been killed so easily in the Smoky Mountain wilderness, but what if something else happened? Especially now that I knew my own mother was a witch also. Surely, she couldn't have been killed so easily as well?

"So, why was I supposed to be kept in the dark?" I was livid by this point.

"You'll have to ask Mamaw."

"But I'm asking *you* now." I gave him a pointed look. "I know you know."

"Fine." He huffed. "You're dad wasn't a witch. From what I understand, he never even knew about us, because you're mom stopped practicing magic after she met him. And since your mom raised you without any knowledge of magic, when our grandparents took you in, they decided to continue with that path. You'd already been through enough when you lost your parents, and they didn't want to add to your shock. Witches start developing the ability to harness magic around sixteen, so they watched you closely for signs you'd inherited the magic genes. When you didn't, she thought it was best to continue keeping you in the dark to shield you from the supernatural world."

"Um, newsflash. That didn't work."

"Obviously." He snorted.

"And she can sense vampires," Aiden revealed with a smirk.

"What? Since when?" He sat up a little straighter. "Since you became one?" It was so weird talking to a family member about what I was now.

"No, I could before. That's what started this mess." I gave him a quick rundown of the last few months and how I ended up becoming a vampire.

"Shit," was all he said.

"Yeah, shit," I agreed.

We all sat in quiet for several minutes. It wasn't the same weighted silence as before, but a contemplative one. It allowed me to stew on everything. And the more I digested it all, the more pissed off I got. The humming started in my chest, and for once, I didn't want it to go away. I *wanted* to embrace my anger. I felt like I deserved to be angry over all this. The sensation went from an irregular pulse to a steady hum, growing stronger with each pissed-off breath I took. It eventually spread out of my chest and down my arms, filling my palms and fingers with heat.

"Riley!" Jeremy barked. "You need to calm the fuck down." I looked over at his horror-filled face.

"You don't get to tell me to calm down. I just found out my whole life was a fucking lie." The heat morphed, feeling like flames were licking my palms. It burned, but felt so good and right all at the same time.

"Seriously, Riley. Listen to him." I jerked my head in Aiden's direction. Seeing a strange mixture of awe and alarm on his face, I glanced down to see what he was looking at. I screeched and jumped up as I saw small flames flickering in my hands. "This whole time you've been a witch," Aiden surmised. "Your powers were just dormant."

"Well, that's just great. How do I turn it off?" I tried furiously blowing on my hands and waving them around, but nothing seemed to affect the small flames.

"Just take deep breaths and calm down," Jeremy coaxed.

I closed my eyes and tried to do just that. After several cycles of in and out, I could feel the burn slowly leave my hands and travel back up my arms, finally disappearing in my chest, where it had all began. I peeked with one eye and sighed in relief when I saw it had worked. I collapsed back in my chair. "I don't understand. I thought when someone was a witch and they were turned into a shifter or a vampire, their powers vanished?"

"Well, you can still sense vampires, so maybe being turned into one triggered the rest of your witch powers?" Aiden offered uncertainly.

"Wait, you can only sense vampires? Has it always only been vampires? Or just since you were turned?"

I considered what he was asking. "Yeah, it's always only been vampires. I was around plenty of werewolves before, and I was never able to sense them like I could a vampire."

"That's odd. I can tell if there's any supernatural near. And I know Mamaw's the same way."

I couldn't stop the eye roll and snort that slipped out. "Well, of course." I threw my hands up in defeat. "There's absolutely nothing that's normal about me."

Aiden and Jeremy both erupted in laughter. "It's not funny." I tried and failed to suppress a grin. It was frustrating not knowing why I was different, but their boisterous laughter was enough to ease some of the tension I was feeling.

"Don't feel bad," Jeremy finally said once he'd sobered enough from his laughing fit. "I guess there's something wrong with the both of us, because I've still been able to sense other supes since I woke up."

"Maybe it's because you haven't shifted yet?" I proposed.

He shook his head. "No, I don't think so. Word on the witch street is that once the shifter virus takes hold, you immediately lose access to all your magic."

"Do you still have yours?" Aiden asked, intrigued.

Jeremy glanced around nervously before he held his hand up. I watched in amazement as the same small flames I'd just freaked out about on my own hands, danced around on his palm. He quickly closed it, snuffing them out as he did.

"Well that's . . . interesting." Aiden glanced between the both of us. "I don't think I'd mention this to anyone else."

"Oh, believe me, I'm not. The only reason I showed you is because Riley clearly trusts you. Even though we're technically on the same team now, if it weren't for that, I never would've even admitted that I was a witch."

"Good," was Aiden's only reply before his phone rang. He looked at the screen and glanced over at us. "I'm going to take this in the hallway. I'll be right back."

I waited until Aiden had closed the door behind him before I scooted closer to Jeremy. Now that all those revelations were out in the open, there was still one more thing that we needed to find out. "Jeremy, I need to know what happened when you were attacked."

He blew out a breath and cocked his head to the side. "It came out of nowhere. I didn't even sense it. One second I was running with my earbuds in, then the next one I was being slammed into by a werewolf. Before I even had time to cast a spell or conjure my fire, he laid into me. He clawed my arms and bit into my side. It was so much pain. I vaguely remember screaming." He paused as he shuddered with the memory. "And then I felt teeth and claws in my legs, my chest, and the pain just overtook me. I'm pretty sure I passed out after that."

I reached over and squeezed his hand. "I'm so sorry this happened to you. I can't even imagine what you went through . . . what you're going through."

"Actually, I think if anyone could be sympathetic to what I'm going through, it's you. I know vampires and werewolves aren't the same, but we were both attacked, and now we're the creature we were attacked by."

"Well, you certainly have a point there," I conceded as I let go of his hand and leaned back in my seat. "But I do have something else I need to ask you."

"That's all I remember," he assured me. "The next time I woke up, I was here."

"No, it's not necessarily about the attack. It's about why you were attacked."

"What do you mean?"

"Well, a few of us went down to investigate the area a couple of hours after it happened, and the werewolf's scent was so faded it couldn't be tracked very far. The Alpha's second in command was one of the people who went with me, and he said it was like it had been days instead of hours. And the only thing he knew of that could disguise a scent like that was a witch's spell or potion."

Realization dawned in Jeremy's eyes. "There *is* a concoction that we start drinking as soon as our magic begins manifesting. It we don't take it, and keep taking it, then other supes would be able to identify us. It keeps us hidden."

"Do you know if it works on others?"

He sunk down in the bed a little. Even though the werewolf virus was running its course through his body, it wasn't full-blown yet, and I could tell he was wearing down. "I honestly have no idea. I mean, I don't see why it wouldn't, but I can't tell you that for certain. What I can tell you is that I don't see any witch willingly giving it to a shifter."

"That's what we were trying to figure out. If this guy stole it from a witch, and this was just a random attack. Or, if he was given the potion by someone who had a grudge."

"Wait." He shook his head. "Are you suggesting that another witch was responsible for this?"

"We have no idea, but we're trying to go over every possible scenario that we can think of. One of them was that if you *were* a witch, could you or someone in the family have pissed another one off so much that they would work with a werewolf to get revenge."

I couldn't read the expression on his face as he stared off into space. After what seemed like an eternity, he pinned me with hard eyes. "My mother isn't the easiest person to get along with. And I won't lie and say that she hasn't done some questionable things in the witching world for her own advancement. She even went as far as marrying a dud witch from a powerful line just for the chance she would get a child that carried those genes. Do you know why?"

I shook my head. I knew even less about witch politics than I did the vampire ones. I'd have to add that to my '*things Riley needs to learn*' list. At the rate I was going, I'd need a five subject notebook to keep track of it all.

"To be able to use me for an ostentatious match." He let that sink in for a moment. I sucked in a deep breath as I realized what he meant. His mom was hoping to use her own son to get connections into a more prestigious family by marrying him off. "It's always been about climbing the social ladder for her. *But* she's never done anything to the extreme that would warrant retaliation such as this."

I contemplated that as Aiden quietly walked back in. "So, you're absolutely sure that a witch wouldn't be working with a werewolf for some type of revenge?" I knew he was, but I had to ask again just to make certain.

"Trust me, she would never do anything stupid enough to risk her one shot at rising in the witching social ranks."

"Okay," I conceded. "Then I guess we have to move forward on the assumption that someone stole the potion from a witch."

"Well," Aiden started slowly, "there's just been another wrench thrown into this."

I looked up at him. He was anxiously standing at the foot of the bed, like he was ready to bolt at any second. "What do you mean?"

"That was Avery. Since the victim of the second attack died, he couldn't get access to the area until very early this morning.

He and the Alpha went down there and found the exact same barely-there scent."

"Okay," I said slowly. "We already figured it would be the same scent. And obviously he still has the potion in his system."

Aiden shook his head. "That's not the problem. They searched a very wide area, and Avery stumbled on another scent that he recognized. This person hadn't taken anything, so it was strong and unquestionable. He tracked it back to the side of a road where they must have gotten into a vehicle and fled. On a hunch, they drove back down to Glendale to your uncle's house and searched again. They went out wider than Avery and Lucian had before and sure enough, there was that same scent that he'd recognized at the second attack site."

"And?" I prompted after Aiden hesitated for too long.

"He's positive the scent belonged to Jessica."

It was a good thing I was already sitting down. "Well, that's just fucking great. If she's working with the werewolf then I think it's pretty safe to assume that Malus is also."

"Yeah," Aiden agreed. "It's too much of a coincidence that we found both of their scents in a matter of days. His near a dead vampire and hers near a shifter attack."

What the hell was going on? So, the drained, dead vampires and the werewolf attacks *were* all connected and orchestrated by Malus. What end game was he actually aiming for? "So, what do we do now?"

"Avery and the Alpha are on their way to *Silver Moon*. They've decided it's time to work together. While they're all in the same room, I think it would be best if they had all the evidence to look over collectively, so I'd like to take the information Jeffrey gave us over there. If you want to stay, I don't mind running it over there by myself."

"No, it's fine. I'll go." There was no way I was going to stay here while there was a rendezvous at the club to figure this shit out and determine a game plan. Besides, I also didn't want to miss a chance to finally meet the Alpha.

CHAPTER 10

T his is all because of our agreement.," he said for the second time. I'd been trying not to stare at the Alpha, but he was so large and imposing, it was difficult not to. Standing at least six and a half feet tall and probably pushing three hundred pounds of pure muscle, he was easily the largest person in the room. Dominance and the demand for submission radiated off of him in waves, making even me want to drop to my knees in obedience.

"And like I said, we'll have to agree to disagree." I had to hand it to Lucian, the Alpha towered over him by about nine inches, but he was holding his own and not showing the slightest signs of acquiescence.

The two stood there locked in an impressive stare-down while the rest of us in Lucian's office waited to see how this played out. Avery was poised with hands clasped behind his back next to his Alpha's side, while Aiden and I sat in the two chairs in front of Lucian's desk. The power from those two rolling through the room was equal parts impressive and scary as hell. Since I was lucky enough to always see the sweet and loving side of Lucian, it was a stark reminder of the formidable vampire he was.

I'm not going to lie, it was also a huge turn on. Part of me wanted to sit back with a bowl of popcorn waiting to see who was going to back down first, and the other part wanted to tackle Lucian on the spot and have him dominate me like I knew he could. Warmth pooled between my legs, and I shifted in my seat to alleviate the sudden desire pulsing in my core.

Four sets of very male eyes suddenly trapped me in their sights. I paused mid-crossing my legs and looked between them, wondering what I'd done to garnish their attention. When I saw the heat flare in Lucian's eyes and the Alpha sniffing the air, my cheeks erupted into mortified flames, and I tried to sink down lower in my chair.

Something to remember about werewolves . . . they had an excellent sense of smell; much better than vampires. So, while Lucian had obviously picked up on my fleeting thoughts of him exerting some of that alpha dominance he was directing toward the Alpha on me, the wolves had smelled my desire. This was just perfect.

Aiden side-eyed me with an amused grin, and I unabashedly elbowed him. A deep chuckle bellowed throughout the room, startling all of us. The Alpha's amber eyes crinkled as his shoulders shook with laughter, obviously finding my embarrassment hilarious. He raised a hand and slapped Lucian on the back. "I think you have your hands full with this one." He bobbed his head in my direction.

"Oh, you have no idea." The seductive smirk Lucian pinned me with only added fuel to the fire burning between my legs.

And only managed to make the Alpha laugh even harder. Avery was even having a hard time maintaining his stony expression.

"Listen, I didn't come here to pin the blame on either one of us. This arrangement we have works. The guys enjoy working for you, and the tension between my wolves and your vampires has never been lower." He took a step back and crossed his arms. "I'm just concerned about what this means and how we're going to take these motherfuckers down."

"I don't disagree, Holden." Lucian began. "And I understand where you're coming from. I'm sure Malus had never seen vampires and shifters working together as a unified unit until we showed up to rescue Riley. But even if that is why he's decided to partner with a wolf now, it doesn't mean he wouldn't have gone that route, eventually. Or that he wouldn't have come back here and tried something else entirely."

Aiden cleared his throat after a pregnant pause. "Don't forget a witch, or at least a witch's spell, is also involved in all of this."

"That's right." Holden uncrossed his arms, only to rest them on his hips. "Avery mentioned something about that while we were trying to track the scent. So, this fucker has all kinds of tricks up his sleeve."

"Unfortunately, that seems to be the case." Lucian mimicked the Alpha's stance. Even though the dominance struggle had thankfully, eased from the room, apparently, they were still subconsciously trying to one up each other up.

"Well, unless we stumble on the rogue wolf's scent while he's nearby, it's not likely we're going to be able to find him. So, what are you all doing about hunting down this Malus asshole?"

I sat back, mostly watching and listening as Lucian and Holden went over everything we already knew and what we suspected was going on, only adding small pieces of information here and there—mainly what I'd just learned from Jeremy, minus the little tidbit about him and I having witch powers. The less people that knew about that, the better. I'd wait until Lucian and I were alone to disclose that little nugget of info.

Once the Alpha was caught up, Aiden handed Lucian the flash drive. He loaded the files Jeffery had placed on it into his computer and scanned over the screenshots with Holden and Avery. Aiden relayed the information we'd learned about all of it from Jeffery, while I was content to remain sitting back and saying as little as possible.

I'd had too many bombshells dropped on me earlier in the day, and there were all sorts of craziness running through my mind. I'd wanted to come along to be in on the planning, but now that I was there, I just couldn't stay focused. I had a feeling that until I spoke with my grandmother, that was going to be my new normal. At least I was able contribute one important thing to the meeting . . . I'd managed to break the tension with my stupid hormones.

"So, it's settled then." Holden clasped his hands together, startling me out of my inner turmoil. "You all try to get an evening set up through the sex ad, and once you have them in custody, we'll take the rest of the players down, one by one."

"I wish it were going to be that simple." Lucian closed the laptop. "This is all assuming that we can pry the whereabouts of Malus, Jessica, the rogue, and whoever else from the people we capture during this ambush."

"If you can't, I guarantee I'll be able to." Holden smiled wickedly, his already amber eyes blazed with a peek of the beast within.

"I may hold you accountable to that offer."

"Please do. It would be my pleasure," he conceded with a growl. "And until these fuckers are caught or killed, if you need our assistance with anything, we're at your disposal. You're better equipped to take the lead on hunting down Malus, so we'll step back and provide help when and where we can."

Lucian stood and shook the Alpha's hand. "I appreciate that Holden. We're going to need all the help we can get."

With that said, Holden and Avery left Lucian's office, so they could round up a pack meeting. He wanted to update all the wolves and warn them to be on the lookout for anything suspicious. Even though Aiden was already aware of everything the Alpha was going to relay to the pack, the meeting was mandatory for all members, so he told me he would meet me back at the apartment once it was over. He followed them out, closing the door behind him.

Alone at last, Lucian stalked over, a predatory gleam in his eyes. I stood, and he wrapped his arms around me, pulling me flush against his body. I felt him harden as he whispered in my ear. "So, you want me to take control?" He firmly grabbed a handful of hair on the back of my head, holding it in place, as he trailed kisses down my jaw and across my neck.

I shuddered, and chills erupted all along my skin from the sensation. Teeth gently scraped my throat, and then his mouth was back at my ear. "You want me to dominate you? To make you mine?" I whimpered with longing and rubbed my thighs together, trying to quell the need blooming in between them.

I was afraid to speak. I knew my voice wouldn't be strong enough, so I merely nodded that yes, I wanted him to do all that and more. Lucian would give me hard and rough if that's what I craved, but he wasn't overly assertive in the bedroom and was more of a tender and compassionate lover—not that I was complaining. It was a nice change to be with someone who cared about my pleasure just as much, if not more than his own.

But seeing his display of power earlier, even though I knew it was only a sampling and more of an *'I won't be pushed around'* warning than anything else, awoke something deep within me that was now sitting up and paying attention. It was making me crave something a little more from him. Something a little more domineering. Something more . . . raw and aggressive.

"You. Are. Already. Mine," he hissed in a guttural voice I barely recognized before pulling my head back and sinking his teeth in my throat. My canines punched down as an unabashed groan escaped my lips. His grip remained firm as he drank me down, and I was helpless to do anything but squirm. I fucking loved it. I guess it was safe to say that the predator in me not only enjoyed being Lucian's prey, but yearned for it.

Lucian and I both went completely still as a knocking reverberated on the door. Lucian groaned with frustration and tenderly removed his fangs. Another shiver vibrated on my skin when he licked the stray blood from my throat. His grip on my hair eased, and I took hold of his sandy waves in return and wrenched his head back, so I could claim his mouth.

We drank each other down as he walked us backward until my legs bumped against the front of his desk, and I braced myself by grabbing the edge with both hands. Lucian left my mouth and made a blazing trail down until he hit the spot he'd just bitten. The puncture marks hadn't completely healed yet, so he teased the sensitive area with his skillful tongue and mouth.

"Lucian," a muffled voice called out, followed by more knocking.

Lucian released an irritated breath and rested his head on my shoulder in defeat. "We'll have to finish this later." He straightened and gave me the full extent of his glowing eyes. "And that's a promise I plan to collect on." That was more than fine by me. I'd never really been into the dominant persona before, but for whatever reason, I sure as hell was today.

I smoothed my hair and took a few calming breaths, so I could let my teeth retract. I was fairly certain whoever insisted on interrupting us knew exactly what was happening on the other side of that door, but I wanted as little evidence as possible. I'd had enough embarrassment for the day when it came to my body's desire for Lucian.

He opened the door, and I couldn't stop the scowl from forming on my face. Of course, it was Bernie who couldn't give us just a few more minutes of privacy, so I could get this new alpha male fantasy out of my system.

Bernie glanced between the both of us several times before he began stuttering about a list of things that needed Lucian's attention. Lucian gave me an apologetic look, but I told him it was fine. Bernie's presence alone was like a bucket of cold water being splashed over my wanton body. Besides, I had something I needed to take care of, sooner rather than later.

"You can make it up to me later," I teased with a wink before I headed out of his office. I didn't look back to see his reaction, but the telltale skip of his heartbeat said it all. He'd make sure all of his obligations were taken care of early tonight, so he could fulfill that fantasy of mine after all.

I couldn't wait.

But before then, I needed to clear my mind and get the answers to the rest of the questions I had. Jeremy was able to enlighten me on so many things, but there was only one person who could finish filling in the gaps. And that person was just who I intended to go and see while I had a few hours to kill.

CHAPTER II

D espite the mixed feelings churning inside me, I was genuinely glad to see my grandmother. She greeted me with open arms, donning her usual summer attire of Bermuda shorts and a light-weight cotton blouse, and ushered me into their old farmhouse. The aroma of peonies filtering in through the open windows mixed with the fading remnants of fried food, filling me with a calming sense of nostalgia. During the spring and summer months, that peculiar combination of fragrances had been a staple in their home for as long as I could remember.

As we sat down across from each other in the living room, she said I had just missed my grandfather, but I already knew he wouldn't be there when I decided to make the trip down. Even though he was retired now, my grandfather couldn't stand the thought of sitting around the house all day, so he made it a point to stay occupied. Whether it was a trip to a local fishing pond, driving to the hardware store to browse for things he didn't need, or venturing over to a neighbor's house to help with a project, he always found an excuse to get out of the house and stay busy. And he wasn't the one I wanted to talk to at the moment, anyway. I'm sure he could've filled in a few of the missing pieces for me, but it was my grandmother who could give me *all* the answers I wanted.

She proceeded to animatedly catch me up on all of the latest town gossip. And as much as I wanted to skip straight to the subject of witches, I knew relaying the newest rumors and not-so-secret scandals made her happy, and I didn't want to take that pleasure away from her. Especially when we were about to have a not-so-delightful conversation about why she decided to lie to me my entire life. And if I was being honest, I was more than a little curious to hear about a girl I despised in school getting caught cheating on her husband with a man more than twice her age.

"This is just such a nice surprise!" she gushed for the third time after finishing her last piece of scandalous gossip. "You stay so busy with your job, I hope you're not neglecting any of your clients by coming down here."

"Not really," I began carefully, as I debated whether I should take Aiden's approach with Jeremy and lay it all out at once, or ease into the topics I drove down there to discuss. Watching her expectant face, so full of love and concern for my well-being, I knew I couldn't bombard her with a series of accusations all at once. Plus, I kind of wanted to see how far she would go to act oblivious about supernaturals—despite the fact that I already knew that *she* knew what I was. And for that matter, also what Jeremy was now.

"I've been busy, but it hasn't been with clients." I let her stew on my loaded admission, and relaxed back in my chair, waiting to see how she would respond.

Several emotions played out on her face before she decided to take the grandmotherly approach. "Oh. Well, I hope you're not letting spending time with your boyfriend get in the way of your job. You've worked so hard to get where you are, I'd hate to see all that hard work go down the drain over a boy."

She quickly added, "Not that I don't approve of him, because I do. He seemed like a well-rounded young man, and it's obvious how happy he makes you." She gave me a warm smile.

"He does make me happy," I agreed. "And I have been spending a lot of time with him. He's been teaching me things that I need to know."

The sudden interest she showed in watching her rings twirl on her fingers spoke much louder than her next words. "Well, that's nice."

When it didn't seem as if she would elaborate on her three-word reply, I chose to delve into another matter of importance. "I went to see Jeremy today."

She gave me her full attention again, her face brightening with hope. "Was he awake? How is he doing?"

"He was awake and doing really good." I weighed my next words wisely. "Laura wasn't very happy with his current condition, but I'm sure you already knew that."

She pinned me with calculating eyes. "Well, of course. Who would be happy that their son was in the hospital after being attacked by a bear?"

It took every ounce of willpower I had to not roll my eyes. I just couldn't fathom why she would keep up this charade, knowing damn good and well that I wasn't even human anymore. It was time to take it up a notch. "You're right, Mamaw. I'm sure anyone in her shoes would be upset." I leaned forward in my seat, resting my elbows on my knees. "But the doctor did come in with some good news while I was there."

Guilt gnawed at me as she regarded me with uncertainty. Technically, I hadn't spoken with the doctor today, but what I was about to say was the truth, regardless. "He said Jeremy's doing really well, and that he'll get to go home in a few days."

"Oh, thank goodness!" She seemed genuinely relieved. "I can't wait to tell your grandfather the news. He'll be so thrilled!"

"Yeah, they're actually kind of amazed at just how well he is doing." She froze, and I suppressed a smirk. "They said they've never seen anything like it. He went from critical condition to almost completely healed in a matter of days."

Mamaw smiled, but it was obviously strained. "Well, that's just all the more to be thankful for." She patted her knees and glanced around the living room. "I was just about to get me a glass of sweet tea, do you want me to get you anything while I'm in the kitchen?"

I wasn't stupid. I knew she was trying to get away from the subject—I'd seen her pull the same avoidance act countless times growing up—but I wasn't going to let her sidestep this that easily. "So, you don't think that's odd?" I pressed. "That he's healing so quickly?"

"Stranger things have happened," she said indifferently and stood from her chair. "Did you want anything from the kitchen?"

I threw my hands up in defeat and growled in frustration. I'd wanted her to tell me everything on her own accord, but I'd seriously overestimated her stubbornness. "Will you please stop acting like you have no idea what's really going on here?" The humming began in my chest, and my gums throbbed, both wanting me to let go of my anger and embrace who I was.

"I have no idea what you're talking about, Riley," she insisted coolly.

The warm purring filled my chest completely, and I let my eyes change. With the enhanced vision I could see her pulse quicken and her body stiffen. "I think you know exactly what I'm talking about. And just to make things clear, Jeremy and I had a nice long chat this morning about our family heritage." Her eyes widened in shock. "I can't believe you all hid the fact that you're witches from me all these years."

She visibly gulped and slowly sat back down in her seat. "Riley," Mamaw began, "I've only ever wanted what's best for you and to protect you. Everything I've done, or kept from you was to do just that."

"So, you thought it was better to lie to me my entire life?"

"I didn't really lie. I just didn't tell you certain things," she insisted with tears in her eyes. "I promise, Riley, if you would've shown any signs of having witching abilities I would've told you everything. But since you didn't, I thought it would best if you didn't know anything about the supernatural world."

The heat spread down my arms, and I was powerless to stop it. Deep down, I knew she would never do anything to intentionally hurt me, and that by keeping me in the dark about our family secret, she truly thought she was protecting me. But the vampire was too close to the surface right then, making it almost impossible to calm down.

I slowly stood and held out my arms, letting the flames ignite in my palms. She gasped, placing a hand over her mouth. "It can't be."

"Obviously, I'm a late bloomer." I glanced down at my hands, expecting to see the same red flames as before, but had to hide my own shock when I observed blue ones dancing against my skin. Seeing the stark difference from the previous time I'd produced them, sobered my anger, allowing me to rein in the vampire instincts, and let my eyes return to their normal hue. As soon as they did, the blue flames blazed to red before vanishing altogether. The heat retreated, quickly travelling back up my arms and into my chest, until the pulsing quieted altogether.

Mamaw cleared her throat. "There's a legend in our family that no one else knows about. Not even other witches. I assume Jeremy told you about our family's special ability to sense other supernatural creatures?"

"Yeah, but he didn't have to tell me about it. I've been able to sense vampires for a while now."

She raised an eyebrow. "Just vampires?" I nodded my confirmation. "And what about being able to conjure fire? Was that before or after you became a vampire?"

"That was after." I filled her in on what had really been happening in my life over the last several months. How I realized I could sense vampires, Malus' obsession with me, my kidnapping, Lucian saving my life, the humming sensation in my chest when I couldn't control my emotions, and finally ending with producing flames in my hands twice that day.

My grandmother didn't say much, only asking a question here and there. Occasionally, she would nod her head, or grip the arm of her chair when I relayed some of the more callous details, but for the most part she sat there and took everything in.

When I finished, she blew out a deep breath, stood, and walked out of the living room. She was only gone a few minutes before returning with two rocks glasses filled halfway with an amber liquid. She handed me one, and I brought it up to my nose for inspection. Bourbon. I'd never been much of a drinker, and neither had she, so I raised an eyebrow in question.

"Don't you give me that look." She huffed as she sat down and took her first gulp. "If ever a situation called for a drink, I'd say it was this one."

She had a point. Even though the bourbon wouldn't affect me like it used to, I raised my glass in a toast to her and took a large drink. With every bite of food I'd tried since I became a vampire tasting so dull, it was a nice surprise to find the bourbon tasted just as I remembered. I almost moaned as it burned its way down my throat. If all alcohol still tasted the same as when I was a human, I'd have to start indulging more often.

After another sip, she sighed. "I'm so sorry you had to find out about everything this way. I should've told you a long time ago. At least then you would've been better prepared against Malus." She set her glass down on the table beside her. "I was just trying to protect you from this world, but I should've known that what's meant to be will happen, regardless of how much you try to stop it. I'm just glad Lucian was able to save you in time."

"So, you're not mad at him for turning me?" I skeptically asked. With the way everyone had talked about the animosity between witches and the other supes, I assumed she would hate him for what he did. Honestly, I'd almost expected her to act differently toward me now as well.

"Are you kidding me?" she asked incredulously. "I'm indebted to him for saving your life. I don't care what he had to turn you into to do it. All that matters is that you're here."

Relief swept through me at hearing those words. I hadn't realized just how much I *had* expected her to look at me differently now that I wasn't human anymore.

"Now, back to our family secret. I always assumed it was just a story passed down through the generations like those old wives' tales you hear, but obviously, there was some truth to it." She finished off the last of her bourbon before placing the empty glass back on the table. "The reason we can sense all supernatural beings is because the ability to turn into them and keep our powers apparently runs through our veins."

"Well, that definitely explains a lot." I finished off my own glass of bourbon in one swig. "Something I didn't mention before . . . Jeremy still has his powers. He showed me the flame-thing this morning."

Her lips set in a firm line. "I'll have to run up there and talk to him about it. The last thing we need is for that mother of his to know about this. She'll exploit it anyway she can."

My phone began ringing. "Sorry." I mumbled as I pulled it out of my pocket. "It's Lucian, but I'll call him back." I sent the call to voicemail and texted him where I was. And I silently cursed as I remembered that I hadn't had a chance to explain most of this to him yet. I'd been careful of what I relayed back at his office, only really saying that Jeremy knew for a fact he wasn't the target of a witch, so the shifter had to have stolen the potion. He still had no idea that my family were witches. I quickly sent another text, telling him that I'd fill him in as soon as I could.

"I still don't understand the blue flames, though," she murmured softly.

I don't think she meant for me to hear that admission, but since I did, I couldn't ignore it. I put my phone back in my pocket and glanced at my grandmother. "So, that's not normal?" Even though I don't know why I even bothered asking, because I already knew the answer. Nothing about me had been normal up until that point, so why would it start now?

She shook her head. "It's got to have something to do with you being a vampire. I noticed when your eyes went back to normal, so did your fire."

That actually made sense. "So, normally, it'll be the same color as any other fire, but if I start vamping out then it turns blue."

"It appears so. But we won't know for sure until we test it further."

I didn't like the sound of that. Letting the fire take over felt good and natural, but it also scared the shit out of me.

She raised up out of her chair and began pacing while talking to herself. "And why would she come into her abilities only after she were turned into a vampire? We'll have to try some simple spells and see if she can do those as well. I still can't believe those family myths are true." She shook her head in disbelief.

I had to agree with her there. Even though I was hearing about this for the first time today, and if Jeremy and I weren't living proof of it, I'd have a hard time believing it was true myself. It did make me wonder what was so special about our blood that allowed us to keep the witch abilities and be either a vampire or a shifter, when no one else could.

I was about to ask her if she knew the reason behind that, when she abruptly stopped. "Of course! Why didn't I put it together sooner? It all makes sense. That has to be the reason for all of it."

"Um, what did you figure out?" I had a feeling I wasn't going to like her answer.

She turned to me with renewed enthusiasm. "The only witch power you had before was the ability to sense vampires, right?" I hesitantly nodded my head. "And then after you were turned, it awakened your witch's fire, correct?" I just stared at her, not sure where she was going with this. "And not only do you have the normal witch's fire like me, you also have blue witch's fire when your vampire instincts come to the surface."

"Well, technically, we don't know that for sure yet," I pointed out.

She continued like I hadn't even said anything, as she walked over to me. "It has to be because of your father."

A chill swept over my body, and I went completely still. "What about my father?"

She sat down next to me on the couch, placing her hands over top mine. "I'm sorry you had to find out this way."

The silence stretched as she tried to find the right words. "Just say it." I finally bit out a little too harshly, but I couldn't help it. I already had an idea of what she was going to say, and I wanted to get it over with. It was an inner debate I'd been waging within myself for far too long, and I needed to know if what I thought about my dad was true or not.

"Riley," she started, her voice laced with sympathy, "your father was a vampire."

CHAPTER 12

My grandmother's confession was almost too much to take in. Wondering if my dad was a vampire was one thing, but knowing for a fact that he was, was completely different. And no matter how much I'd been leaning toward the idea that he could've been one, it still didn't prepare me for the shock of having it confirmed. Especially now that I also knew my mother was a witch, and I'd never really been human at all.

I was probably the first vampire-witch crossbreed to exist, and I wasn't sure how I felt about that. It sounded much more badass than it actually was. Before I'd been turned, I only had one simple witch power and the rest of me was nothing spectacular. No one, especially in my school gym classes, would have ever thought I was anything other than an average human. Hell, my own witch grandmother never even suspected that there was anything special about me.

But for some reason, all that changed when Lucian gave me his blood. My grandmother and I both believe that was somehow the catalyst to trigger my dormant powers. And since I was only twenty-four, and Born vampires could go through their Becoming—the transition from mostly human to full vampire—up until the age of twenty-five, there was a chance that I would've ended up a vampire anyways, and my witch powers were just lying in wait until that moment. But, that was a moot point. We'd never really know if that were the case or not since Lucian had to turn me before we had the chance to see if I'd go through the Becoming on my own.

I stayed at my grandmother's house for a couple of hours after her admission and discussed that possibility and everything else in much more length. She acknowledged her initial fears of my mother dating a vampire, but once she met my father, all her doubts were erased. Apparently, they were crazy about each other. And since Mamaw had felt the same way about my very human grandfather—and went against her own Coven to marry him—she didn't want to stand in the way of true love.

No one else in the family besides her and my grandfather knew about my father. Considering how Jeremey's mother had always been, my own mother decided it was best to maintain the charade that my father was completely human and oblivious to the supernatural world around them. They didn't know what I would become, and they didn't want anyone, whether it was other witches or vampires, to know that I'd been born.

Since my uncle had no powers, whatsoever, he couldn't sense other supernaturals like my mother and grandmother could. Laura didn't have the ability, so unless they were told, there was never a risk of anyone finding out. Jeremy was only eleven when my parents disappeared, and wouldn't gain access to the sensing power, along with his other witch abilities, for another five years, so he was also clueless. There were only four people who knew about me, and they'd wanted to keep it that way.

Mamaw said it was such a relief to finally be able to talk to me about all of it. And it was a little unnerving to hear her confess that once I turned sixteen, she'd been so worried that one day she would walk into the house, and I was either going to be casting fireballs, or withering on the floor, changing into a vampire.

And the whole keeping me away from the supernatural world? That was because she suspected foul play with my parents. She said that despite being half human, my mother was a very powerful witch. And even though my father had always been tight-lipped about his family and where he came from, she knew he was a Born vampire and formidable in his own right. There was no way they would've gotten lost hiking, or died from an animal attack. She knew something wasn't right with the whole situation and even though she had no proof, she suspected it had something to do with vampires. She was afraid that if I knew the truth, I'd go out looking for them and get myself killed.

So, naturally, when Lucian went down to their house with me to meet them, she'd been nervous when she sensed him in the vehicle. My parents had been adamant about keeping my true origins a secret, and since she suspected vampires in their disappearance, me suddenly bringing one home seemed suspicious. But one look at the two of us together, and she could tell it was the real deal, just like my parents, so she welcomed him and acted as if she had no idea what he was.

She wanted to ask me if I knew he was a vampire, but she knew if she did, it would open a door to questions she wasn't prepared to answer. And when she saw me at the hospital and realized I'd become a vampire, she assumed I'd been turned. Because if I'd went through the Becoming on my own, it would mean one or both of my parents had been vampires, and I would've been calling her to find out how that was possible. Since I was still clueless about my heritage, she thought it would be best to keep it that way, and to do that, she needed to act like she had no idea that I wasn't human anymore.

"Hey," Lucian greeted me and leaned down for quick kiss.

I waited until he was situated next to me on my couch before I began my explanation. "Lucian, I'm so sorry that I bailed on you last night. So much happened yesterday between Jeremy and my grandmother, and I just needed some time to process all of it."

I'd been so overwhelmed with the influx of revelations the day before that I'd called Lucian on my way home and asked to be alone that night. When I got home, Aiden still wasn't back from the pack meeting, and for once, I was glad he wasn't there. I didn't want to talk to anyone. I wanted to drink my nightly blood bag and wallow in my inner turmoil alone.

"Riley, you don't have to explain yourself to me. I can only imagine what you and your family are going through with Jeremy's attack. Just because I've been a vampire for a long time, doesn't mean I can't sympathize with that." He cupped the side of my face with one of his hands, gently rubbing his thumb in a caressing pattern. "You've been going non-stop since it happened, and I understand if you need time to process it all."

Not for the first time, I wondered how I'd gotten so lucky to have him in my life. Maybe I was way overthinking the '*date like normal people*' plan and should wholeheartedly embrace our connection, and how my heart and body wanted nothing to do with the '*taking things slow*' strategy. I sighed, closing my eyes, and leaned into his touch. I breathed in his musky scent and fought the urge to release my teeth and sink them into his flesh.

This was the exact reason I hadn't wanted him to come over the night before. I wanted to stew in my self-misery, and dissect both conversations I'd had with Jeremy and Mamaw with a sharp, non-distracted mind. With the prospect of finishing what we started at Lucian's office still so fresh in the back of my mind, there was no way I could've resisted the urge to do just that and completely ignore everything I'd just learned. Lucian's presence had a tendency to be equal parts calming and instant aphrodisiac, and my traitorous body would respond to both with no questions asked.

I felt his lips brush against mine, sending a trembling thrill through my body. He cupped the other side of my face, deepening the kiss and scooting closer to me, as he did. It was slow and sensual and nothing like the dominant version of him I'd experienced the day before. As much of a turn on that was and as much as I'd still like to play out that little fantasy that I never knew I had, this was the version of Lucian that I'd fallen in love with and yearned for in every ounce of my being.

But, this was also not the time to get carried away and give into what my body wanted. It was already late in the afternoon, and Aiden would be back soon with Jimmy for our first movie marathon night since I'd moved back into my apartment. And I needed to fill Lucian in on everything I'd discovered before they got there. Aiden already knew what Jeremy had disclosed, but I hadn't told him what I'd learned from my grandmother.

It didn't seem right to tell Aiden before Lucian; I wanted Lucian to be the first one to know about my true origins. And even though I trusted Aiden with my life, this was a secret that my parents didn't even want my own uncle to know, so I had to be very careful with who I entrusted the knowledge with. Eventually, I would tell Aiden, but I needed a little more time before I was ready to divulge those secrets to him.

"Wait." I broke the kiss and placed a firm hand on Lucian's chest. "There's some things that I need to tell you."

He dropped his hands and leaned back, searching my face—and probably my thoughts—for a clue to what was obviously bothering me. I kept my mind blank. I'd rather verbally tell him than him gather the pieces from my thoughts.

"Okay." He shifted on the couch until he was facing me completely. "What's going on? Is this about your cousin?"

"Partly. I learned a lot of interesting things yesterday between him and my grandmother."

Curiosity bloomed in his eyes. "And?" he prodded.

I blew out a deep breath. Here went nothing. I just hoped he wouldn't look at me any differently once he knew the truth. "Jeremy *is* a witch, but like I said yesterday, he's absolutely sure that he or his mother, who's also a witch, hasn't done anything to piss off any of the others. Or at least not to the extent that would justify sending a werewolf after him."

Lucian didn't seem surprised. He merely nodded and said, "I thought that could've been the case." After I frowned at him expectantly, he elaborated. "After smelling his blood, I knew he had to have taken the witch potion that makes the scent bland to vampires. There's only one logical explanation for that. And since witches are born to other witches, I assumed his mother was one also. Although, honestly I'm surprised she would've married a human. They're usually all about species purity and won't take the chance that their children won't be witches as well."

I averted my eyes. Laura had taken a chance, but it wasn't as great of a gamble as Lucian was thinking. "That's not all."

"You're referring to something you learned from your grandmother?"

I pulled my knees up to my chest and hugged my legs tight. Once I had enough courage gathered, I looked him straight in the eyes and nodded. "She's also a witch."

Confusion bloomed on his face. "But, you weren't a witch?" It wasn't a statement. Now that he knew where I came from, he was doubting himself.

"Technically?" I asked. "I don't know what I was." I let that admission hang in the air for a moment before inquiring, "Did you know that some witch families have extra abilities like some vampires have extra gifts?"

"No, I just assumed some were better at some things than others. I've seen witches who couldn't pull off anything more complex than simple parlor tricks, but I've heard about others who had boundless power. There've been rumors of great psychics, witches that could control the wind, and I even heard about one that could freeze a man where he stood."

"Well, apparently, every witch has access to the basics, general spellcasting and potion making. But some of the older, more powerful families have gifts that are passed through the generations. My family was blessed, or I guess cursed, depending on how you look at it, with a few of them. One of them is the ability to sense other supernaturals."

Lucian laughed, like Aiden had the day before when he found out the same thing. I guess I was the only one who didn't find it funny. "So, all along you being able to sense vampires was because you're a witch?" He shook his head. "Unbelievable. And to think, I had no idea a witch line carried that kind of power." Slowly, the smile began slipping. "Wait, but that doesn't make sense." He sat straighter. "Why can you still sense vampires?"

"That's the tricky part." I admitted and went on to explain the rest of my family's secrets; retaining the witch powers if turned into a vampire or a shifter, how I'd been able to produce a flame twice the day before, I even explained how my mother was only part-witch and I simply said my father wasn't one—I'd delve into that after I got all the witch stuff out of the way. I even confessed that Jeremy still had his powers, but I made Lucian promise he wouldn't utter a word about that to anyone.

He agreed and listened in complete fascination to everything I said. "Riley, I'm speechless," He finally stated after I was finished. "I can't stress enough, however, that you can't let anyone else know. Vampires have tried to gain witching powers for longer than I've been alive, and if the key to success is in your blood, there are some that would stop at nothing to get access to you and drain you dry."

I gulped. My parents had wanted the knowledge of my existence kept a secret, but I'd assumed it was because either side would be pissed that they were together and had a child, or that I'd become a vampire in a witch family, or vice versa if I'd been raised by my father's family. I hadn't even considered the idea that it was because I could've successfully inherited both the vampire and witch genes, essentially making me a crossbreed between the two species. And if that were the case, then people would be after me, so they could replicate the phenomena.

"Well, that's still not all." I lowered my legs, crossing them and rested my hands in my lap.

Lucian immediately reached over and encased them with his. "Riley, it's okay. I don't think anything you have left to say could top the fact that a witch line can be turned into a hybrid with other supernaturals."

I snorted and let out a nervous giggle. "Um, so me and my grandmother have a theory about why I'm a little different."

"You mean why you can only sense vampires?"

"Yeah, and the fact that my flame started *after* you turned me." I wet my lips uneasily. It wasn't that I felt like I couldn't trust him with this, it was just hard to admit it to someone. He squeezed my hands and gave me a reassuring smile. "I told you my father wasn't a witch, but I didn't tell you that he also wasn't human." Lucian went unnaturally still. "He was a vampire."

His emerald eyes bore into mine, the silvery luminescence swirling through them, battling to take over. I quickly continued, "When you gave me your blood, it mixed with my weird crossbreed genes and not only turned me into a vampire, but triggered the dormant witch powers to awaken as well."

I watched as the war raged within his eyes, until finally the vampire subsided, and they returned to his normal hue. "While it's rare for a vampire and a human to conceive a child together, it does happen, but I've never heard of it being achievable with another species." He shook his head. "I don't know if that's because no one has ever tried with the others, or because it's never been possible before. But honestly, I'd put money on the fact that being able to procreate with a vampire is limited to your family. If they could be turned into a vampire and retain their powers, then there's obviously something that allows your line to successfully meld with us."

As soon as I realized he wasn't going to freak out about this, I relaxed. "At least this explains why nothing about me has been normal or made sense since all this started."

He chuckled, and I glared at him, a little annoyed that my abnormality amused him. "Riley," he began, but heavy footsteps sounding on the staircase outside my apartment, halted whatever he was about to say.

Hearing a familiar laugh, I smiled. "It's the boys." As much as I wanted to hear what Lucian's reply was, I wasn't mad for this interruption. I'd been looking forward to movie night, just like old times, for a while. I'd even already ordered pizza for delivery and had Aiden pick up a couple boxes of popcorn while he was out. It was just what I needed to distract my mind from all the craziness that had, and still was, happening that week.

Lucian leaned forward and whispered, "Listen, for now I don't want anyone else to know about all this. I know Aiden already knows some of it, but until Malus is captured, I think it would be best if the full extent of your lineage stays between the two of us."

Since I'd already had a similar debate with myself, I was more than willing to agree. Especially since I hadn't fully realized the consequences of what could happen if the wrong people found out. "Okay," I agreed. The last thing I needed was for the news that I was born to a witch and a vampire get out while Malus was on the loose and nearby.

Aiden and Jimmy came barging in the door, and I didn't even try to suppress the grin on my face at seeing them. Especially when I noticed they were matching today. Both sported blue t-shirts, distressed dark denim jeans, and worn brown work boots. The boots were a staple in their wardrobe, and I had no idea how they survived wearing them daily. It was pushing a hundred degrees outside, and yet, there they were, barely breaking a sweat. "Hey, guys!"

They greeted us with the same genuine enthusiasm, and I wondered if they'd missed our movie and game nights just as much as I had. Aiden's dimples magnified when the doorbell rang to the office downstairs. "Well, that was perfect timing. I'll go down and get the pizza."

"I already paid online. And that's including the tip." I called after him as he raced down the stairs to the office.

"I think he may be hungry. Are you not feeding him?" Lucian joked.

"Ha, you know better than that."

Jimmy set a couple of grocery bags on the kitchen counter before sitting down in the chair next to the couch. "I don't know, I think Lucian's on to something. I think he's already lost a few pounds since he moved back in this week."

I rolled my eyes and threw the closest couch pillow I could reach at him. Of course, he caught it easily. "Hey, how'd you know I wanted a pillow?" He tucked it behind him and leaned back, crossing his ankles and placing his hands behind his head. "Ah, thanks, Riley."

Lucian's phone dinged. He tossed me a worried glance before he pulled it out. I knew what he was thinking . . . this wouldn't be the first time he'd been called away from one of these nights, leaving me, Aiden, and Jimmy to enjoy it without him. I hoped that wasn't the case tonight. He'd been working non-stop over the last week, and I knew these next few hours were going to be a much-needed reprieve from that for him.

"Bernie just wanted to text me an update on the second werewolf attack."

Jimmy perked up at the mention of the rogue shifter. "Oh, yeah?"

Lucian nodded. "He says they released the name of the second victim."

"Ugh, I knew I was forgetting something." I threw up my hands in frustration. "I'm so sorry, Lucian. With everything else that Jeremy and I talked about yesterday, I completely forgot to ask him if he knew the two vampires that were murdered."

"It's fine," he insisted. "We know the same person is behind all the attacks now, and it's not like you still can't ask him tomorrow. I doubt knowing if there's a connection between the victims will make a huge difference anymore."

He had a point. Malus was the connecting factor with all the attacks. And who really knew how he was picking his targets?

Lucian focused back on his phone. "Riley, you actually might know the victim. He says it was a twenty-four-year old male originally from Elizabethtown." Another text came through. "Ah, here's the name. It was Trevor Clark."

Chills immobilized my body. Not only did I know Trevor, I'd dated him. He was the only serious boyfriend I'd ever had. We'd dated for a little over two years, but I broke up with him when I found out he was cheating on me while we attended different colleges.

Lucian's head jerked toward me. "Your ex-boyfriend?"

Jimmy sat up, looking between the two of us. "You used to date the second victim?"

"Yeah, but that was several years ago. We were high school sweethearts, but broke up when we were in college."

"Riley, I hate to say this, but I don't think it's a coincidence that you know both attack victims." Lucian stated bluntly.

I racked my brain for any reason it could be just a coincidence, but I came up with nothing.

"I know you don't want to hear this, but I think he's right. We know Malus is behind the attacks, so both wolf victims being linked to you couldn't have been an accident," Jimmy, who was usually always joking and rarely ever serious, said firmly and without any hint of his typical playfulness.

"But, we stopped dating like six years ago. Hell, I haven't even seen the guy for a good two years." I was grabbing for straws, and I knew it. It didn't matter that he was loosely connected to me. For Malus, that was probably a bonus. It would keep me guessing if he actually was targeting people I loved, or in Trevor's case once loved, or if all of it was just a big coincidence.

"You have to assume that every attack, every move is calculated and for a specific reason to get to his desired end game." I hated to admit it, but Lucian was probably right. And I think the main reason I didn't want to acknowledge it, was because that would mean Trevor's death was on my hands.

It didn't matter that I wasn't the one who attacked him, it was because of me that he was killed. And just because we hadn't been together for a long time, it didn't mean that I wished anything bad to happen to him. Besides his habit of straying outside of committed relationships, he was a good guy. His dad had bailed on Trevor, his mom, and younger brother and sister when Trevor was twelve, and he did everything he could to help his mom out. He worked a part time job in high school to help pay the bills and put his younger siblings to bed every night, so his mother could work a second part-time job in the evenings.

"I agree," Aiden said, pulling me out of my thoughts. I don't know how long I'd dazed out, but apparently, he'd come back up from getting the pizza, and the three of them had made a decision about something. "I think we should do it tonight. And as long as you're okay with it, we can even still do movie night there." He grinned at me. "That way Riley won't have anything to complain about."

"Hey!" I protested, even though I had no idea why I should be offended.

"Well, what do you say, Riley?" Lucian stood and all three of them stared at me expectantly.

"Um," I blushed. "What do I say about what?"

His eyes sparkled with amusement. "I said, now that we know Malus is at least targeting people you know with the wolf attacks, you should probably move back to *Silver Moon* until this is over." I glanced at Aiden. "You both should stay at the club," he further clarified. "Malus is clearly trying to send a message. And I'm afraid he'll come after you again."

As much as I wanted to demand that I was a kickass crossbreed and could take care of myself, I knew that was a big, fat lie. Yeah, I was a witch-vampire hybrid, but until I learned how to use the abilities and powers that came with that title, I was far from kickass. And I knew I couldn't hold my own against a centuries old vampire. At the rate of non-learning I was doing, I'd be lucky if I could even take on a newby vamp like Jessica.

No, unfortunately I knew my place in the power hierarchy, and for once, I wasn't going to argue with Lucian. But that didn't mean I wasn't going to have stipulations. "Okay. But as long as this doesn't interfere with movie nights."

Lucian laughed. "I think I can manage that."

CHAPTER 13

L ucian's Sire was and wasn't what I expected. Like all vampires, Sebastian was strikingly attractive. He had dark hair styled haphazardly, what appeared to be dark eyes, and a few day's-worth of stubble on a strong jawline. I could only see him from the waist up, but he wore a charcoal suit jacket, opened to display a crisp vest of the same color and a blueish dress shirt. The top buttons were undone and spread open, adding to his *'I want to look like I don't care, but actually I tried really hard to accomplish this'* look. I guess I now knew where Lucian got his style from. I'd seen the exact same look countless times when he worked during club hours.

What I didn't expect about Sebastian, however, was the fact that he didn't seem to be the normal dickish vampire and actually cared about what was going on in his territory. I'd been anticipating something more along the lines of Brianna, and while he did come off a bit cocky at times, he reminded me more of Lucian than anyone else. Maybe Lucian inherited a little more than just fashion tips from his Sire.

"I'm warning you," Sebastian began, "you need to be very careful when they arrive." Unlike Lucian's faint, barely there version, he had a refined British accent.

"I will," Lucian confirmed, and I suppressed a grin. The longer he spoke with Sebastian, the more pronounced his own accent was becoming again. It was something I think we all did. While there were plenty of southern accents in Louisville, mine had almost completely disappeared since I'd moved up here. But anytime I went home for a visit, or even just spoke with my grandparents on the phone for any length of time, mine did the same thing and would become more distinct for a little while afterwards.

"Good. Greyson couldn't tell me much, so I have no idea how deep the treachery runs. All I know is that his father saw Malus sneaking out of a private entrance to the Low Council member's private wing. Obviously, his own father isn't involved, but for all they know, all six of the other members could be in on it."

This was just great. Sebastian had requested Lucian to setup a video call with him first thing that morning because he had something important to tell him. Despite our late night, Aiden and I were just about to leave to head over to the office, so we could finish up the last bit of paperwork that was left before the opening, when Lucian asked if I wanted to be included on the call. Obviously, I wasn't going to pass up the opportunity to see the man who'd turned Lucian into a vampire during the beginning of the Victorian era.

Sebastian was good friends with one of the seven Low Council member's sons, Greyson, and had received a tip from him about Malus. Greyson's father, like four of the other members, were also House Heads of their own vampire Houses. He'd been leaving the Low Council's headquarters after a recent session to take care of business back at his own House when he saw Malus leaving the council's private wing. Since Malus was a hot topic recently because of what he did here in Louisville, he instantly recognized who he was.

He had no way of knowing which Council member was obviously working with Malus, so he hadn't spoken to anyone about what he saw, not sure who he could even trust. When Sebastian expedited the request to have BloodGuard assistance in this region because of two vampire deaths and signs that Malus was back and involved, he immediately reached out to his son, Greyson, to relay the warning for Sebastian. Someone on the Low Council was working with Malus.

"And I can't stress to you enough the importance of keeping this quiet. If anyone found out that his father relayed this information to Greyson, or that he in turn told me, it wouldn't end well for any of us." His dark eyes shot over in my direction. "Lucian assures me you can be trusted, but I know a Blackwell when I see one." He leaned closer to his computer's camera. "I don't know how you're related, but if Knox Blackwell so much as smirks at Greyson or his father, I'm going to assume you're the one who leaked the information."

Panicked, I looked to Lucian. "Blackwell?"

Lucian shook his head. "Sebastian, we've been over this. She doesn't even know our politics, let alone a Council Member." He glanced at me quickly before focusing on Sebastian again. "Regardless of how much she favors the Blackwell line."

Blackwell line? "My father's surname was Hunter. I've never even heard of anyone with the last name Blackwell." I knew whatever I said would do little to erase any doubts in Sebastian's mind, but I wanted him to know the truth. Or at least what I thought was the truth. After everything I'd learned this week, it was probably a safe bet to question everything I thought I knew to be facts about my life.

"And his given name?"

"Drake. His name was Drake Hunter."

Sebastian smirked. "Drake Hunter, huh? And exactly how old are you?"

I swallowed hard. I didn't like the sudden interest Sebastian was taking in me. "I'm twenty-four."

He barked out a laugh and leaned back in his chair. "Like I said, Lucian trusts you, and that's good enough for me. However, if Knox finds out about this, you will be the first person I hunt down for answers."

I nodded my understanding. I knew this Knox Blackwell guy wouldn't hear anything from me, but for my sake, I just had to hope he didn't hear anything from anybody else, either. No big deal. Just check off another mark on my list of complications lately.

Lucian rolled his eyes. "You're being a bit dramatic, don't you think?"

My mouth hung open as I watched Sebastian for a reaction. He didn't seem like the type of person who appreciated someone talking back to him. When his mouth spread into a huge grin, I wondered if I had him totally pegged wrong.

"Is there any other way to be, old friend?" Sebastian chuckled.

"For you? Not likely." Lucian smiled genuinely.

Sebastian looked off to the side of the camera and gave a quick nod. "I'm afraid I'll have to end this call a little sooner than I'd planned, so I'll make this quick." He waited until we heard a door close before continuing. "I did get confirmation that they'll be there either tonight or tomorrow morning. They couldn't spare a BloodGuard unit of four, so it should just be two of them. I have no idea where they're coming from, but that's of no consequence. What does matter is that the Low Council are the ones who control the BloodGuard. So, like I've already said, you need to be very careful when they get there. For all we know, they could end up aiding Malus instead of capturing him."

"I understand. I'll warn everyone to be cautious and report any suspicious behavior to me immediately."

"Good. And if they ask why then grow a pair and tell them you're the fucking Consul, and it's none of their bloody business."

I couldn't stop the chuckle from slipping out. It was obvious he knew Lucian all too well. Don't get me wrong, Lucian did an amazing job as the local Consul, and could obviously hold his own during a power show—ala the incident with the Alpha— but he did have a tendency to be a little easy-going and indulgent. If someone asked why, he would try to think of an excuse, or a reason why he was asking them to do what he wanted. Telling them to just do it because he said so would never even cross his mind.

"Anything else, *Sire?*" Lucian asked with a smirk.

Sebastian narrowed his eyes. That had clearly hit a sore spot. I wondered if he didn't like being referred to as Sire. From the way I'd overheard other vampires talking, it wasn't unnatural to call the person who turned you either Sire or simply by their name. I guess it depended on the relationship between the two? I'd never called Lucian Sire, and he'd never asked me to. And honestly, I don't think I would even if he wanted me to. I'd stick to Lucian, whether he liked it or not.

"I would like you to keep me updated. But other than that? No. That will be all, for now." He pushed his chair back, but before ending the call added, "Oh, and Riley? Just some food for your thought. Draken Blackwell, the heir to the Blackwell line, vanished from House Blackwell about thirty years ago. And no one has seen him since." With that said, the screen went black.

His insinuation wasn't lost on me. Draken went missing thirty years ago and my father, Drake, had met my mother probably around twenty-eight years ago. While it seemed like a stretch, at this point I wouldn't cross anything off as impossible.

"I apologize about Sebastian. He's an interesting character."

"It's fine Lucian." And it was. As long as Sebastian was on our side for this showdown with Malus, that's all that mattered to me, because we were going to need all the help we could get. And if he was right about Draken Blackwell, then I'd owe him big time for pointing me in the right direction of finally finding out where my father came from.

Speaking of. "What do you know about Draken Blackwell? Or the Blackwell line?"

His shoulders went rigid. "The Blackwell line is one of the older Born families. They can trace their vampire lineage back several generations. I don't know their exact history, but I know House Blackwell has been in existence for over a thousand years." He avoided eye contact as he closed the laptop on the coffee table. "The original House Blackwell is still in England, run by Leopold Blackwell. His son, Knox, runs the American House Blackwell in New York. He's also one of the seven members of the Low Council of Northern America."

"And Draken Blackwell?" I prodded.

"I honestly don't know much about Draken. I've never belonged to a House, so I don't keep up with House politics. I only make a point to be aware of who current House Heads are." He sighed heavily and leaned back against the couch. "Sebastian would be the person you need to speak with about Draken."

"Why is that?"

"Because he used to be a member of House Blackwell."

Yeah, like that didn't open up a can of worms. "Was that before he turned you?"

"Yes. No. Both." He rubbed ran a hand through his hair. "He was Housed, but he left after he Made me." He stood quickly. "I've only met Knox once, but I'll never forget his eyes." Lucian glanced down at me. "Your eyes." Picking up the laptop, he walked out of room.

I was speechless. I'd already assumed Sebastian's comment was referencing my eyes, but Lucian's reaction was peculiar. It was obvious he didn't want to talk about being turned—he never had before. I'd brought it up a few times, and he'd always avoided the subject. But now I wondered if the Blackwells also had something to do with it. The more mysterious the circumstances surrounding his turning became, the more I wanted to know what actually went down. But since it was a topic Lucian clearly did not want to discuss, I tried not to push it.

Lucian walked back in the living room, stopping in front of me with a hand held out. "Once all of this is over with Malus, I can setup a meeting with Sebastian, if you'd like. He may be able to help you figure out if Draken Blackwell is Drake Hunter."

I placed my hand in his and allowed him to help me stand from the couch. Sebastian was intimidating, but Lucian didn't seem intimidated or frightened of his threats, so maybe I'd take him up on that offer. "I'd like that. As long as you're there with me."

"Of course." He leaned down and gave me a chaste kiss. "I guess I need to round up a meeting with the security team to warn them about being cautious when the BloodGuard gets here. It'd probably be a good idea to include Ellie and the other bartenders as well." He paused. "Actually, I think I'll include the donors, too. All of them will be around the BloodGuard, so they should all be prepared."

"That sounds like a good plan." I gave him one more kiss before leaving his basement apartment and searching for wherever Aiden had gone. The last thing on my mind right then was work, but all we needed was just a few more hours, and everything should be ready for next week. Let's just hope we made it that long.

CHAPTER 14

W hen I woke the next morning, I felt different. I couldn't quite put my finger on what that difference was, but I knew something wasn't right. There was an underlying edginess, almost like the calm before the storm, but I had no idea why it was there. It probably didn't help that I was starving. My throat burned with need, and I tried to remember when I'd last had blood.

I was almost positive I'd had a bag the night before. Aiden and I had managed to get everything finished and ready to go for the re-opening next Wednesday, well before nightfall. Since Jimmy wasn't working at the club, we decided to have another movie night. It was a Friday, and Lucian was busy upstairs, so it was just the three of us in Lucian's basement apartment. And yes, I distinctly remembered heating up a bag in between *The Princess Bride* and *The Goonies*. We'd decided on having a classic eighties movie marathon.

I was always hungry in the mornings, but this was borderline ravenous. I pried myself out from underneath Lucian's arm and made my way into the kitchen. Two blood bags later, and I still couldn't make my teeth retract. I sighed and got out another one. I couldn't remember ever needing this much blood at once, other than right after my turning.

Lucian came padding in as I downed my third glass. "Something's wrong with me." I admitted. "I just drank three bags. And honestly? I think I could go for another one."

His lip twitched as he got four bags out and placed them in the microwave. "Tomorrow is the blood moon, so you're going to need a little more blood for the next three days."

How could I have forgotten that? "Aiden mentioned something about the blood moon the other day. He said it affected all supernaturals, but he didn't know exactly what it did to vampires. I've been wanting to ask you about it, but I guess with everything going on, it just kept slipping my mind."

He leaned against the counter as we waited for the blood to heat up, and I had to covertly wipe my mouth to check and make sure I wasn't drooling. His sandy waves were tousled from sleep, and all he wore was a pair of jogging pants that barely hung onto his hips. Lucian wasn't excessively bulky, but his muscles were well-defined, and all I wanted to do in that moment was run my hands over them.

The microwave dinged, causing me to jump, and Lucian let out a hearty laugh. He retrieved the bags, opened the first one and filled my glass. "We aren't controlled by the moon like shifters are so it doesn't affect us as severely. But we do get hyped up from it."

"'Hyped up?'" Was that the weird feeling I was having?

He downed his first glass, and re-filled it with another bag before elaborating. "Our senses are heightened, and the vampire is closer to the surface during a blood moon. It will be harder to suppress your natural instincts, and your body is going to crave more blood."

Sounded like the perfect time to have a homicidal vampire and a rogue werewolf out on the loose. "Am I going to be okay to be around Hattie tomorrow? I've bailed on her so many times, I'd hate to have to cancel again."

"You said it would be around noon, right?"

"Yeah, and I'm sure she wouldn't stay longer than a couple of hours." I sipped my glass, thankful I could sip this one slowly and savor the taste.

"You've amazed me this week with how strong your control is. As long as you're not around her closer to the evening, I think you'll be alright. Although, I doubt Aiden will be able to be there. Most of the wolves will be going down to pack land today in preparation for it. I think the ones working tonight are going to head down there as soon as we close the club."

"I figured. Aiden already said pretty much the same thing." I was fairly confident I could handle myself, but the last thing I wanted was to put Hattie in danger. Especially if that danger was me. I'd wait and see how on edge I was in the morning before I made a definite decision either way.

Lucian's phone began ringing in his pocket. I hadn't checked the time when I woke up, so I wasn't sure exactly how early it was, but I wasn't surprised. He had to make sure his phone was on him at all times because he received texts and calls at all hours of the night and day. "Lucian," he answered.

I heard Bernie's voice on the other end, so I figured I'd go ahead and take my shower and get ready for the day. His calls tended to last longer than I wanted to stand around waiting for it to end. And since I was officially ready for my office to re-open, I'd offered to hang around the club and help Lucian out for the day. So, I might as well make good on that offer and be ready to get started when he was done taking care of business. I rinsed my glass in the sink and headed back to the bedroom.

∞ ∞ ∞

Three hours later, I found myself congregated on the dance floor space with Lucian, Bernie, Avery, Ellie, Alex, Brianna, Aiden, and a few other vampires that I could never remember their names. Bernie had made contact with the person who had the online ad that our two dead vampires had responded to, and we were having an impromptu meeting on where to go from there.

The person answering the ad wanted to set up the rendezvous at someone else's house and the only logical choice was Bernie's rental home. Malus would immediately recognize my address, Lucian said he had another home in the city—which was news to me—but since Malus could've easily found out that information he didn't want to use it, and the rest of the vampires lived in apartments. Lucian was afraid that would either make it difficult to capture the vampires involved in this, or innocent humans in the apartment buildings would get hurt in the process.

Bernie didn't seem too thrilled at the idea, but he agreed without a fight. And now that we had a location and a time later that night, we needed to figure out who was going to be there and who would stay behind for a summer Saturday night at one of most popular clubs in Louisville. Since a lot of the wolves who normally worked security were already out of the city, preparing for the upcoming blood moon, we were going to be stretched thin.

"I'll stay here," Ellie volunteered, which seemed out of character for her. I would've thought she'd want to get in on the action, but she'd seemed a little distant and distracted the last few days, so maybe it had something to do with that.

"I know four of the stronger wolves are staying to work." Avery glanced at Brianna. "If you're okay with being in charge of security tonight, I can help with the take-down."

"That's fine with me," Brianna agreed. "And I've already called all the vampires who are on rotation for full moon back up. With the four wolves, we should be operating at full capacity."

"Good." Lucian nodded. "Now we need someone to be in the house. It obviously has to be a vampire, or they'll be suspicious. And it can't be me because I'm sure Malus has already made them aware of my scent."

Alex raised his hand. "I'll do it."

"Are you sure? We know there were three of them the last time, and you'd be alone with them for several minutes while we get into position to take them into custody. If they suspect anything, they could turn on you." Lucian walked closer to Alex. "This is probably the most dangerous job tonight."

"I'm positive," Alex confirmed resolutely.

"I can tend the bar with Ellie tonight," one of the other female vampires offered.

Slowly, the rest volunteered for various things, whether it was working the donor rooms in the VIP area, waitressing in the sections where the couches and tables were, or even just hanging out to make sure no more help was needed. Bernie was going to stay behind and oversee the workers. And since I refused to be left behind at the club with Brianna while all this went down, Aiden volunteered to go with me.

"So, that gives us Alex as the bait, two wolves, and since the two BloodGuard should be here before then, three vampires to take these guys down. If my suspicions are correct and Malus won't be there, then that's six against three." Lucian looked between Alex and the two wolves. "I don't know about you all, but I'm content with those odds."

I kept doing the math in my head, but I couldn't come up to the same number of vampires that Lucian had. "What about me?"

He glanced at me before turning to the crowd. "That's all, everyone. Thank you for coming and for taking on additional roles tonight."

Everyone who wasn't involved in capturing the vampires, except for Ellie and Bernie, quickly disbanded. Lucian came over to me. "You will stay in the vehicle while the two BloodGuards, Avery, Aiden, and myself capture these guys."

I opened my mouth to protest, but Ellie stepped in. "When are the BloodGuard going to be here?"

As if on cue, the tingling sensation erupted on my arms. "Um, I think they're already here." Ellie's eyes widened, and we all turned toward the doors that led to the front of the club. It wasn't long before heavy footsteps sounded, and the double doors were thrown open, two huge men sauntering in.

Both were well over six feet tall and wore a variation of essentially the same outfit, which consisted of black jeans, t-shirt, leather jacket, and sunglasses. The one on the left had a clean-shaven face, shoulder-length dirty blonde hair, and a smirk. The other had dark hair buzzed close to his head, the stubbled outlining of a beard, and if I had to put money it, a perpetual scowl.

"Well, I'll be damned," the one on the left said as he removed his sunglasses. "Ellie, is that you?"

I twisted to look at her, wondering how the hell she would know these guys, but the space where she'd been was empty. I searched until I found her all the way across the room, about to go through the door to the stockroom. She stopped, and slowly came back over, grimacing. I glanced at Lucian, but his face was a mask. If he knew what was going on, he wasn't letting it show.

"Everette," She acknowledged the guy.

"Is this where you've been hiding all these years?" He slid his sunglasses in his shirt pocket, a huge grin plastered on his face. "Wait till I tell Kade. He's going to flip out."

She narrowed her eyes. "If I wanted that asshole to know where I was, I would've told him myself."

His brow bunched down in confusion. "Are you still pissed about that dumb bitch at the House?" Ellie's only reply was a snort, so he crossed his arms and added, "You know it wasn't what it looked like."

She held up a hand. "Just stop. I didn't want to hear any excuses then, and I don't want to hear them now."

"Fair enough," Everette said. "But just so you know, we've been assigned to the same BloodGuard unit since the beginning, and he's never stopped looking for you."

Silence stretched as Ellie and Everette stared each other down. I was equal parts intrigued as hell with this conversation, and feeling like I was intruding on something private. The other BloodGuard was the one who finally broke the quiet, his voice booming through the club. "We didn't come here to get Kade's old piece of ass back. We've got a job to do, so let's do it."

Ellie was in Everette's face before I could blink, fangs bared. "You'd better not tell him I'm here." She whirled on the other BloodGuard. "And you're an asshole." With that she stormed off.

"It was good to see you, too, Ellie!" Everette called after her, laughing.

The other guy just looked bored.

"I take it you're from House Bordeaux?" Lucian crossed his arms.

"I am," Everette confirmed. "But Gavin's from House Moretti in Chicago." He jerked a thumb toward his partner. "And I take it you're Lucian?"

"I am." He glanced around the dance floor, noticing more than one nosy eavesdropper hanging around at the edges, trying to get a good look at the BloodGuard men. "Why don't we go to my office, and I'll fill you both in on everything that's been going on?"

"Sounds good to me." He motioned to Lucian. "Lead the way."

We all stepped in behind Lucian, and it only took a moment before Everette was at my side. "And you are?" He gave me a flirtatious smile.

"Riley."

"Well, Riley, it's a pleasure to meet you. If I knew such beautiful vampires were in Louisville, I would've come here a long time ago." He winked.

Oh, he was one of *those* guys. The ones who flirted and hit on every girl they met, a regular horndog. I'd dealt with plenty of those types in my life. And I was trying to think of how to reply, when Lucian was suddenly in between us. "Riley," he bit out, "is off limits to you."

"Whoa, dude." Everette put his hands up and took a step back. I couldn't see Lucian's face because he'd strategically placed himself in front of me, but I was pretty sure he'd vamped out. "I'm sorry, I didn't realize she was yours."

"Well, now you know." He grabbed my hand and continued walking. "Don't let it happen again," he warned over his shoulder.

I couldn't believe it. Was Lucian jealous? And staking a claim on me? I didn't know if I should be thankful for him putting on end to Everette's flirtations, so I wouldn't have to deal with them, pissed that he didn't think I could reject him on my own, or flattered that Lucian was declaring I was his. I'd have to think this one through and decide how I felt about it later.

As we entered the door to the employees only hallway, I heard Gavin chuckle and say, "Maybe that'll teach you to keep your dick in your pants for a change."

I suppressed a giggle and risked a peek at Lucian. The smug smile said it all, he'd put Everette in his place, and he was glad everyone knew it.

We all piled into Lucian's office, except for Bernie, and I wondered where he'd slithered off to. I still hadn't had that talk with Lucian about him yet. I needed to quit putting it off. I knew

Lucian trusted him, but I just got a weird feeling from Bernie. And I'd feel better once I voiced those concerns to Lucian.

Once everyone was situated, Lucian clapped his hands together. "Okay, so let's fill Everette and Gavin in, and then we'll make our plan for tonight."

For the next few hours, that's what we did. No one left until there was a solid plan in place. It sounded fool proof, but I knew all too well how plans could fall apart when Malus was involved.

CHAPTER 15

There was a buzz in the air, making me antsy as we sat in the vehicle. I think we all felt it when we went left the club to head over to Bernie's rental home, everyone having a little extra pep in their step. I had yet to figure out if it was because of the blood moon, or the thrill of getting one step closer tonight at finally ending this with Malus. Either way, we were all pumped up and ready for whatever came our way.

Bernie lived in a surprisingly nice neighborhood. I don't know what I was expecting, but I guess it was something more along the lines of dark, damp, and creepy . . . to match his personality. But he lived in a nice suburban neighborhood, his house being a modest brick with probably at least three decent-sized bedrooms. I didn't know how much Aiden was paying him, but I knew there was no way it was enough to afford this place—not to mention the fact that he probably hadn't even gotten a paycheck yet. So, that left me to the conclusion that old Bernie already had some money before moving down here.

Alex was already in Bernie's house, impatiently waiting for these guys to show up. Avery, Aiden, and Everette had gone one street over and used the darkness to cross through the yard behind Bernie's house. If all went well, the three of them should be strategically placed at the rear of Bernie's yard, waiting for Lucian's signal to enter the house through the back door.

Lucian, Gavin, and I were in Lucian's vehicle, parked on the side of the road a few houses down from Bernie's. The plan was for the two of them to go in through the front door once whoever was supposed to meet up with Alex went inside the house. Lucian would text Avery right before they went in, so between the five of them, all the exits would be covered.

I was supposed to stay in the vehicle like a good little vampire.

We'd been waiting for over an hour, but if our guys were punctual, then they should be pulling up any minute. In all that time being cooped up in a vehicle with Gavin, I hadn't learned very much about him. He barely spoke, and that was usually only when asked a direct question. And I'm pretty sure I nailed it on the head when I decided the scowl he wore when entering the club was a near permanent one. So far, I'd barely seen him crack a smile and only heard him laugh once when Lucian had put Everette in his flirty place. He was the epitome of tall, dark, and moody.

Everette, on the other hand, was the complete opposite of Gavin. While we, or should I say they, were planning this stakeout earlier, Gavin was clearly in his element and was one of the major voices in the decision making. And it wasn't long before it was apparent that flirting and joking around was just his personality. We were all still leery of divulging in or trusting either one of them too much, but I could tell that it wouldn't take long before everyone warmed up to him. I just hoped it wasn't a part of some bigger plan involving Malus. What perfect way to get our guard down than by trusting these two, only to have them turn on us at the last minute.

The three of us sat up a little straighter as a vehicle that looked suspiciously like the one we'd seen on the street camera slowly drove past us. I held my breath until it carefully pulled into Bernie's driveway. Lucian quickly sent a text to Avery, letting him know to be ready.

"Do you have all your weapons?" I already knew they did, but it didn't hurt to double check. We were fairly certain these guys were just peons, and probably newly turned, carrying out Malus' wishes, but it was better to be safe than sorry.

Lucian had changed into a dark t-shirt and jeans to blend into the night before we left. And he added to his ensemble, a custom holster strapped around his shoulder, which held a hand gun and a knife. He said he wasn't planning on using them, but just in case Malus showed up, he'd rather be prepared.

We could heal a lot of injuries. Just how much, I had no idea. Fortunately, I hadn't had to test out just how good our healing ability was. But, I did know that a few bullet or stab wounds wouldn't kill us, and we could heal them quickly. Vampires weren't as allergic to silver as shifters were, but the allergy was still there, and if the wounds were inflicted by something containing silver, it would take us longer to heal them. So, Lucian made sure his knife and bullets were made of pure silver.

"Gun is loaded, and the knife is easily accessible." Lucian gave me a weak smile. He knew I was worried.

I turned around to Gavin. "How about you?" He grunted and nodded his head. He had a holster strapped over both shoulders, each one containing a pistol. And I knew from watching them prepare before we left that he also had at least three knives hidden somewhere on his person. "And the handcuffs?"

One good thing about having the BloodGuard with us was they had nifty silver handcuffs with some type of spell-work embedded in them, making them near-impossible for a vampire or shifter to break them. Apparently, there's one witch line out there that makes them for the BloodGuard and any shifter packs who can pay the steep price for them. I guess making a small fortune on those spelled cuffs far outweighed any reservations they had about working with other supernaturals.

Gavin pulled two pairs out, one from each pocket, to show me he had them, before stuffing them back in his pants. "Everette also has two sets on him. And if we need more, I've got some in my bag." He patted a black duffel bag resting beside him in the back seat.

"They're going in." Lucian eyes were fixed on Bernie's house. "We were right. There's three of them." He picked up his phone, placing the final text to Avery, letting him know that Lucian and Gavin were headed up to the house. He set the phone down on the console, and leaned over it, giving me a searing a kiss. "Hopefully this won't take long," he whispered against my mouth.

He glanced back at Gavin. "Let's go." He exited the vehicle, but before closing the door, bent over and demanded, "Stay in the vehicle, Riley."

I crossed my arms and tried not to pout. I knew I wasn't as skilled as the rest of the guys going in that house, but being told to stay in the vehicle while the big boys handled business, only pissed me off. The humming in my chest began, and I cursed silently. The last thing I needed was to attract attention because I couldn't put flames from my hands out.

I felt something tap against my arm. Looking down to see what it was, I was shocked. Gavin was slipping me an extra knife from his bag. I gently accepted it, but when I tried to say thank you, he held up a single finger to his lips, and nodded in the direction that Lucian was standing, waiting on him. I nodded and simply offered a smile instead as a token of my gratitude. He might not have been inviting me into the action, but he was sending me a message. One that said he thought I could handle myself and needed a weapon just like the rest of them.

Maybe I'd been a little too quick to judge Gavin. But as he left the vehicle, I buried that thought. Until we knew for sure if they were compromised, I couldn't let either one of them grow on me. I needed to keep my guard up.

So, I sat back, gripping my knife and watched the scene unfold. I could see Aiden dart through the backyard, getting closer to the house. Lucian and Gavin swiftly ran to the front door and after only a moment of hesitation, burst through it. I turned the keys on long enough to crack my window. Lucian had left the front door open, so I wanted to see if I could hear what was going on in the house.

There were some shouts of surprise, scuffling sounds, and more than one item was knocked over. Thankfully, I knew they were faint enough that only another supernatural could hear them. But a sudden cry of pain had me on edge. I recognized that voice. It was Avery.

A growl bellowed out of the house that sent chills down my spine. The last time I heard that sound, I'd been in the middle of a fight between vampires and fully shifted werewolves. Someone else, possibly Alex hissed with pain, and another was thrown on the floor with a thud. Then an unfamiliar vampire was running out the front door.

I tightened my grip on the knife and placed another hand on the door handle, ready to bolt after him. He ran toward my direction, but I hesitated, expecting Lucian, or one of the others to come running out after him. Lucian had warned me to stay in the vehicle, but it would only take a few more seconds for this guy to get far enough away that someone chasing after him from the house wouldn't be able to catch him.

He streaked past me, and I made the split-second decision to pursue him. No one else was coming after him, and I didn't want any of these assholes to get away and warn Malus. Pushing the door open, I clung to the knife, and raced after him.

As he continued to gain a lead, I was thankful he was stupidly sticking to the road for this chase. If he was smart, he would've cut into someone's back yard by now, where it would've been easier to use obstacles to slow me down—not that he needed too much help in that department. I was also thankful that it was a little past eleven at night, so most of the lights were out in the houses we were sprinting past. I didn't want to add '*dealing with human police*' to our list of problems tonight.

When we turned a corner, and I saw where he was heading, I knew I needed to catch up fast. There was a fenced in playground up ahead, and while the fence wasn't a ridiculous eight-foot monstrosity like the one I scaled in Old Louisville, it was a good five feet tall, and I was going to have trouble getting over it as quickly as I needed to.

Remembering I'd only managed to vault over the wrought iron fence when I let my vampire slip to the surface, I decided to do just that now. My vision enhanced, my canines shot down, and I was suddenly filled with another burst of energy. Pushing my legs harder and faster, I was surprised that it was actually working. Little by little, the distance between us was closing. And the fact that I wasn't even out of breath was just as amazing as the idea that I might be able to catch him.

I could almost reach out and touch the guy when we came up to the fence. He leapt right over, not even using the fence itself as leverage. What. The. Fuck? Maybe we were wrong to assume these were newly turned peons?

Not having any time to react, I mimicked his move and crossed my fingers for luck as I pushed off the ground and launched in the air. My eyes widened when I was able to clear the fence as easily as he had. The escapee landed unsteadily, and that moment of hesitation allowed me to land on his back, just as he was about to take off running again.

The momentum rolled us both for several feet, and I lost my grip on the knife. I quickly jumped up, spying it right by my opponent. He obviously hadn't noticed it, because instead of going for the knife, he got to his feet and lunged for me instead, fangs bared.

Something inside of me shifted, and time slowed down. As he came at me, I sidestepped, extended an arm straight out, and clothes-lined the guy. He didn't stay down for long, though, and came at me a second time with a frustrated growl. This time, I didn't have time to dodge him. He barreled into me, knocking me flat on my back.

His hands immediately went to my throat and remembering my old self-defense classes from when I first moved up to Louisville, I wrapped my legs around his waist, using all my strength and a slight tilt to the left first, before using his own weight to swing him over to the right and off of me. Luckily for me, he wasn't a large guy. He probably only had an inch or two of height and about thirty pounds on me. If he'd been much larger, I'm not sure if that move would've worked.

Taken by surprise, he released my throat as we switched positions. I adjusted my legs, grabbed the knife—which was right beside us now—and ended up straddling him. With the knife against his throat before he realized what the fuck had just happened and how I was able to turn the tables, I bared my own fangs. "Don't you dare move one fucking muscle, or I swear I'll slit your throat." It was a bluff. Unless it was a '*my life or his*' situation, I couldn't do something like that. But he didn't know that. And I was hoping my performance was enough to convince him I would do it.

He gulped, the knife biting into his Adam's apple. I watched as the vampire glow left his eyes, and acceptance filled them. It wasn't long before I heard two sets of footsteps. I was afraid to take my eyes off of him, so I waited until they were closer and inhaled deeply, trying to catch a scent from them. Some of the tension in my shoulders eased as I recognized one of them as Lucian.

"Riley, are you okay?" he asked frantically. I nodded my head, keeping my eyes and the knife fixed on man beneath me.

"Seriously?" Everette asked, as I heard them jump the fence. "Look at her. She's a total badass." He chuckled. "Why the hell did you make her wait in the vehicle? We could've used her back there at the house." He came up next to us and lightly kicked the guy in his arm. "Then this douchebag wouldn't have gotten past us."

I heard the clinking of handcuffs, and only then did I slowly remove the knife from his throat and let my eyes bleed back to normal. I was too high on adrenaline to make my teeth slide back up, but since it was just us vampires out there, I wasn't worried about them being on display. Lucian helped me up, embracing me tightly in his arms. "When we went after him, and I saw you weren't in the vehicle anymore, I panicked." He gave a forced laugh. "I should've known you wouldn't listen to me."

"I'm sorry, Lucian. I saw him getting away, and I just couldn't let that happen."

He pulled back enough to look at me. "You don't have to apologize. I just didn't want you to get hurt." Lucian glanced at Everette putting the handcuffs on the guy. "But, obviously, I underestimated you."

I wasn't going to admit that I was just as surprised at how that went down as he was. No, I'd take the compliment. But I'd also make sure I started training with him or someone else soon, so I could start earning that badass crossbreed title. Because even though I felt like a badass tonight, I knew I was far from it. Luck had more to do with me capturing him than any legitimate skills. "So, what happened back there? How did he escape?"

"I hate to break this up," Everette jerked the guy forward, "but we really need to get out of here before Malus realizes they failed."

"Agreed." Lucian brushed his lips against mine. "I'll tell you what happened on the way to the club." He took a step back and grasped my hand. "Come on. The sooner we can interrogate them, the sooner we can find out where Malus is."

He didn't have to tell me twice. I followed behind them but kept an eye on our surroundings. Tonight seemed just a little too easy. The entire trip back to the vehicle, I kept waiting for the ball to drop and someone jump out and attack us.

CHAPTER 16

W e snuck in the back of *Silver Moon* and went straight downstairs to the basement. There were several dorm-like rooms down there with a bedroom, bathroom, and a mini-kitchen, living room combo. They were a place for whoever, whether it was a vampire or werewolf, to stay for the night, or even if they needed to use it as temporary housing while they were in between homes.

Each captive was placed in a separate non-inhabited room, with Avery, Aiden, and Alex guarding the doorways. Lucian and the two BloodGuards rotated through the three rooms, interrogating each one individually. My body was still buzzing with excitement, so while they did that, I went to Lucian's apartment and downed two glasses of blood.

I had a feeling my idea of interrogating people differed greatly from theirs, so I was content to stay where I was, browsing my neglected social media accounts, until they were finished. But I did leave the door to the apartment cracked, just in case they decided to congregate in the hallway to discuss whatever they were able to find out. Just because I didn't want to be involved with the questioning, didn't mean I didn't want to know the answers.

Lucian had filled me in on the way over to the club on what happened in the house. Basically, it was barely contained chaos and didn't go according to plan at all. The three guys had taken some type of short sword into the house to do the same thing to Alex as they had done to the other victims. When Lucian and Gavin barged through the front door, the one that I chased down grabbed it and went on the defense.

The addition of Avery, Aiden, and Everette only escalated things. Gavin was adamant that they were Housed vampires, from the very House he was originally from before joining the BloodGuard, so while they didn't seem like experienced fighters, they were Born and naturally stronger and more agile than a Made vampire. While trying to subdue the two who were weaponless, my guy slashed out and tried to cut anyone he could.

Avoiding him, Lucian and Aiden managed to get and hold down the other two, so the BloodGuard could handcuff them. During that, my guy was able to slice Avery's arm, and put a gash across Alex's chest. He then threw the short sword at Lucian, barely missing him, and knocked Everette to the floor. While he ran out of the house, Aiden switched gears, trying desperately to calm down a ready-to-turn-furry Avery, and Lucian and the BloodGuard put their captives in the back of Lucian's Land Rover. Gavin stayed with them, while Lucian and Everette tracked me and the slasher down.

After a solid hour, I grew tired of reading political rants and scrolling through pictures of what people had eaten for dinner, so I switched it up and started reading a book I'd downloaded a month ago but hadn't had time to start on yet. I moved over to one of the armchairs, pulling my legs up in the seat, and settled in for a chance to get lost in someone else's life for a little while.

I was almost a quarter of the way through the book when I heard shuffling from the hallway and a heavy door open and close. "Are you sure you don't need me to go with you?" I recognized Aiden's voice.

"No, I'm good," Avery snarled in a growly voice. "Get some rest, and I'll see you down there tomorrow." Weighty footsteps retreated farther down the hallway.

After another hushed discussion I strained to decipher, Lucian, Aiden, Everette, and Gavin came into the apartment, settling down in the chairs and couch situated near me. I sat up in my own and looked between them all expectantly. "Where are Alex and Avery?"

"The sword they had was made of silver. Avery's cut was deep enough to give him a good taste of it, and with the blood moon tomorrow, it was taking every bit of willpower he had not to fully shift. He didn't want to do that here, just in case he couldn't cage the animal again until after the moon tomorrow night." Aiden leaned back on the couch he shared with Lucian, crossing one leg over the other. "So, he's driving down to pack land now, that way if the wolf slips out, he'll already be there."

"Alex went up to find a donor, so he could heal his silver injury faster." Lucian fixed his gaze on the two BloodGuards sitting across from him. "Once we're done here, you both are more than welcome to take the vein of any of the donors here. Or, there are plenty of blood bags, if you would prefer those."

"He'll take some bags." Everette pointed toward Gavin. "But, I prefer vein if I can get it." He flashed fangs, grinning at the prospect of biting into someone he didn't know. I suppressed a shudder at the thought, and seriously hoped I never got to the point where I preferred biting people over bags of blood.

Gavin crossed his arms, glaring at Everette. "You'll take bags tonight. We need to get them up to House Moretti asap. The sooner we get them up there, the faster we can get back down here."

"Fine." Everette sighed heavily. "I'll take a bag to go for now. But when we get back, I'll take you up on that donor offer."

"That's fine," Lucian agreed. "How long will the transport take? I'd like this resolved with Malus as soon as possible. And now that we're back to square one . . .," he trailed off.

"Wait." I held up my hand. "I don't understand. What do you mean, back to square one? And where are they getting transported?"

The three of them—well, really it was Lucian and Everette, with only a comment or two from Gavin—explained what they were able to learn from the interrogations. Aiden had already heard most of it from being right there while it was happening, so he sat there quietly, letting the others fill me in.

As Gavin had insisted before, all three were from his former House in Chicago. They were younger, between the ages of eighteen and twenty. And each one insisted they'd never even heard of Malus, let alone were they working for him.

They argued that they were acting on their own accord to murder vampires down here. Apparently, taking Made vampire heads as trophies was some sort of sick hazing ritual where they were from. They each needed one, so Alex would've been their last, and then they were going to head back to Chicago. When I side-eyed Gavin after that revelation, he insisted it wasn't something they all did. He claimed that he'd never even heard of it before.

The more they relayed, the more I started to understand the hatred and hostility that the Made and unHoused vampires had toward the Born and Housed ones. Especially when it came to these guys. They were the children of members of the House Council, and were the epitome of privileged little shits. And the practice of decapitating others? That was reserved for the elite members of House Moretti as a *'welcome to adult vampirehood'* tradition and was hush-hush to the lesser Housed vampires. At least that's what the one I chased down, which I've dubbed Slasher, was insisting.

So, the three of them headed outside of their own region to fulfill their atrocious custom. They were told it couldn't be close to the House, but since they wouldn't be able to take decapitated heads in carry-on bags, they chose somewhere they could drive to in less than a day. Louisville, only being a five or six hour drive to Chicago and boasting an ever-growing vampire population, seemed like the best choice for them.

Slasher and crew set up the online sex-wanted ad to attract, what they assumed would be, lonely and easily taken down vampires. They went to the victim's house, took turns drinking from the target to make them weaker, and when they were least expecting it, sliced off their head. When the job was finished, they took their trophy, keeping them iced in coolers back at their hotel room.

The whole purpose of this sick practice, according to Slasher, was to prove to the House elders that they were capable of doing whatever was necessary for the better good of the House. It was an ancient tradition passed down through the generations and was a coming-of-age trial. Back in the day, they would place the heads on a spike in front of the House as a warning to anyone who would go against them. In the modern times, as soon as the deed was done, and the House elders saw the proof, the heads were discarded like trash.

The entire thing made me sick.

But Slasher was also adamant that we couldn't touch them over their crimes. Being the children of House Council members, they were exempt from any repercussions of their actions. They weren't even remorseful for what they did, only that they didn't get the third head to take back.

When I questioned how accurate that was, the response was a unanimous yes. Since they were Housed, it fell back to the House BloodGuard to carry out any type of punishment, regardless of what region they committed the crime in. If we tried to extract retribution from these guys, and didn't let the House take care of their own, it would rain down a bunch of shit from the higher ups that we weren't prepared for, or willing to, to deal with.

To say I was furious, would be a major understatement. And we couldn't afford for the BloodGuard to find out about me, so it took everything I had to rein the rage in and not let my witch fire loose.

Our previous plan had been to capture the bad guys and grill them for information on their ring leader, Malus. They would tell us what his ultimate goal was and lead us to his hiding place.

Now, like Lucian said, we were back to square one. And nothing made sense again.

Aiden got a whiff of Malus' scent near the second victim's house, and Avery had found Jessica's near both werewolf attack sites. So, was it all just a coincidence? Or were Malus and Jessica only working with the shifter, and him being in PRP that day was the only coincidence?

With everything we thought we knew up in the air, the new plan was for Everette and Gavin to drive the Housed back to Chicago as soon as we were finished discussing all this, and they had some blood. They would deliver them to the House BloodGuard, where I was sure Slasher and his two friends would barely get a slap on the wrist for murdering two of our vampires, and then Everette and Gavin would come back down here. We would regroup tomorrow evening to figure out where to go from there.

Gavin and Everette seemed to think the best way to push forward was for them to scour the areas where the scents were found to see if they could find anything. But I could tell Lucian was skeptical. We still didn't know if we could trust these two, so why would we let them go looking for Malus alone? But it was clear they were used to doing what they wanted and that they really didn't need Lucian's permission to go about this however they saw fit. They were including him in on the planning as a formality.

I knew the BloodGuard answered to the Low Council and not a Consul, or even a Dominus, but I would've thought Lucian had the final say when it came to running an investigation in his region. It was just another thing that I didn't understand about the way vampires ran things. And since there was nothing I could do about it, I tried not to dwell on it.

"My main concern is the blood moon tomorrow." Lucian stood, walking Everette and Gavin to the door. "We have to work on the assumption that Malus *is* controlling the wolf attacks. And if that's the case, there's no telling what he has planned for tomorrow night."

"Don't worry, we'll be back way before nightfall. And Gavin and I will go out searching for any signs of the rogue or Malus." Lucian didn't seem convinced, and it didn't go unnoticed. "Look, if anything happens, all you have to do is call, and we'll head right over to wherever there's trouble."

With that said, the three of them left, so Lucian could round them up some blood before their trip, leaving me and Aiden by ourselves. I waited until I couldn't hear them anymore before turning to him. "What do you think about all this?"

"Honestly?" He blew out a deep breath. "I have no fucking clue."

"You're not the only one," I agreed with a snort.

"I mean, I believe what those vamps said. I really don't think they have any connections to Malus, and it was just a twisted chance that all this went down at the same time." Aiden shrugged.

I sat back, contemplating everything we'd learned tonight. "So, you do think he's controlling the rogue?"

"Without a doubt. The Alpha and Avery smelled Jessica *with* the rogue. And if she's with him, then you know Malus is behind it."

"That makes sense." And it also made sense when it came to the victims. I had never met the two decapitated vampires, but

I knew both of the people who were attacked by the werewolf. But that still left the question of why Malus was in PRP that day? Unless he'd been following me. But surely, if that was the case, we'd have noticed him before, right?

"I think I'm going to crash here tonight. I'm exhausted." He stood, stretching. "My car's back at the office. Do you mind if I ride over there with you tomorrow when you meet Hattie?"

"Sure, I don't mind at all. Are you going to be okay, though? I thought you needed to get to pack land before then?"

He reached a hand out, helping me stand. I didn't realize just how exhausted I was until then. It was true that I didn't need as much sleep as I used to, but between spending so much time out during the day this week, and all the excitement from earlier, I was more than ready for bed.

"I think I'll be fine until then. I may even be able to stay with you for a little bit if you need me to. But it won't be for too long."

I gave him a hug. "What would I do without you?" He was like the brother I'd never had, and I was so grateful to have him in my life. And not for the first time, I wondered how in the hell was he still single? Oh well, some girl out there's loss was my gain.

"Probably get into even more trouble than you do now." He chuckled.

Pulling back, I grinned, "I can't argue with you there."

"Get some rest," Aiden called over his shoulder as he left the apartment for his own room in the basement. "You're gonna need it to get through tomorrow."

I wasn't going to argue with that, either. If what I'd experienced tonight was just a sampling of how the moon was going to affect me tomorrow, then I was going to need more than rest. I'd need equal amounts willpower and sheer luck.

CHAPTER 17

The humming in my chest had been my constant companion since I woke up that morning. And it was increasingly difficult to keep my teeth in check. The buzzing energy that seemed to be in the air the night before, was an unbridled entity unto itself today. And since it was only almost noon, I knew it was just the beginning of it.

Hattie wasn't going to be happy, but there was no way I could spend an entire afternoon with her. I was going to be lucky to make it an hour or two. I didn't think I'd be tempted to attack her, but keeping myself from vamping out was going to be a problem. If all the other vampires felt the same way I did, it was a good thing it was Sunday and the club was closed tonight, because otherwise, the partygoers would've assumed they'd stepped into a surprise costume night at *Silver Moon*.

Jeremy had called first thing that morning, letting me know he was being released from the hospital, and into the care of the Alpha. Even though Jeremy wouldn't be able to shift for the first time until the moon was full in the sky, Holden wanted him, and all the other wolves, down on pack land before it was even close to nightfall. Jeremy admitted he was nervous, but assured me he would be fine.

"Well, that's odd." I pulled up to the gate behind my building, but no one was in the guard box to let us in. The tenants weren't given any type of remote access on the assumption a guard would always be posted to open and close the gate. No guard, no access.

"I spoke to George a few days ago," Aiden said, opening the Jeep door. "He said he was pulling doubles all weekend." He proceeded to walk around the locked guard box, sniffing the air. Once he made a few rotations, amber eyes found mine, and he shrugged.

I felt bad for Aiden. What I was experiencing was nothing compared to him. All morning, amber and blue fought in waves to win control of his eyes. The wolf was there, barely below the surface, and it was a visible struggle for him to keep the human at the forefront. I knew he wanted to let go; to let his inner beast out.

I knew because I wanted the same thing. That was the main reason I was a nervous wreck right then. My vampire wanted out, to be free and unchained for a change. It felt so good when I could be my true self without fear of someone seeing me, or getting carried away in bloodlust. Vamping out was my true self now, suppressing that was only a ruse to hide amongst the humans.

Werewolves were a dual species, just as much human as they were wolf. So, while it was perfectly normal for them to be in their human form, it was just as much of a release for them to shift as it was for vampires to embrace their true nature.

203

"He was here, but the scent is a couple of hours old," Aiden said as he climbed back in the Jeep. "Maybe something came up, and the company hasn't been able to get a replacement over here yet."

That was plausible, but for some reason just didn't sit right with me. Uneasiness filled me, and I had no idea why. "I guess." I backed up and headed around to the front of the building. "But that doesn't help us get to your car." Which was currently parked in the gated lot.

"Yeah," Aiden sighed, with a pained expression. "I can hold out a little longer until George, or whoever else gets back."

I shook my head. "What if it takes a couple of hours? You can't do that to yourself."

"I won't really have a choice."

"Why don't you take my vehicle?" Aiden began to protest, but I cut him off. "You can drive mine down there, and I'll text Lucian to have someone come and pick me up when I'm ready."

He thought it over. "I guess that would work. You sure you don't mind?"

"I don't mind at all."

"Okay," Aiden agreed. "But I'll go ahead and go inside for about thirty minutes. If a security guard isn't back by then, I'll take your Jeep."

"Deal." As I neared the entrance to my building's front parking area, I saw Hattie's familiar black Mustang parked and waiting for me.

"Thanks Riley." Aiden slid his sunglasses on, careful to hide the evidence of his inner turmoil. "You ready for this?"

"No. Yes." I parked next to her car, and leaned back in my seat. "But here goes nothing."

All three of us got out of the vehicles at the same time, Hattie immediately coming over to give me a long overdue hug. "So, is this man candy the infamous Lucian?" she asked unabashedly.

"No, this is Aiden." I laughed, pulling back and gesturing toward him. "He's my friend and co-worker."

Aiden's appreciative smile was one I'd seen countless times on men when they were in Hattie's presence. She was a couple of inches shorter than my five-foot-five frame, but where I was all curves and borderline chunky, Hattie was petite. Throw in rich brown eyes, shoulder-length chestnut hair, delicate, feminine facial features, and some curves in her own right, and she was a total knockout.

"Hey, it's nice to meet you." Aiden offered his hand.

"Same here." She flashed her best flirtatious smile.

I rolled my eyes. "Aiden's not going to stay long. He just needed to grab some things before heading over to his parent's house." The lie rolled off my tongue smoothly.

"Oh, well that's a shame." Hattie pouted.

I knew that look also. Hattie was interested. I quickly grabbed her by the arm, leading her away from Aiden and toward the front door to the office. I loved Hattie with all my heart, but her track record with men wasn't good, and I didn't want Aiden to get hurt. And unfortunately, that's all that waited for him if Hattie was involved. She blew through men like a stripper during a dollar dance.

Once inside, my hand hovered over the keypad for the security system, wondering why it wasn't beeping at me. Aiden closed and locked the door back behind him. "What's wrong?"

"I guess I forgot to set the alarm the last time we left." I could've sworn I'd set it, though.

"We *were* in a hurry," Aiden pointed out. And I had to admit that he was right. The last time we'd been here was when I found out my ex was the second werewolf attack victim. Aiden and I'd hastily packed, so we'd still have time to watch a movie or two at *Silver Moon* before he and Jimmy needed to turn in. Unlike us, shifters needed just as much sleep as humans did.

Hattie let Aiden lead the way up to my apartment, and I knew it was only, so she could have a good look at his ass walking up the stairs. Especially when she insisted to go up after him, making me bring up the rear.

I pushed my sunglasses on top of my head and flicked her in the butt. She turned and glared down at me, mouthing, "What?"

"You know what!" I silently mouthed back, pointing a finger at her, then at Aiden.

Hattie burst out laughing. When she ran into Aiden, almost falling backward down the stairs, I couldn't hold back my own snigger of laughter. She glared down at me, which only made me laugh harder.

"Go back down." Aiden turned suddenly. "Now!"

Before I could even process what he was saying, the door to my apartment swung open. A tall, burly beast of a man held up a gun and shot three times into Aiden's back. Hattie screamed as Aiden fell forward onto her. I caught both of them . . . barely, and silently thanked whoever was listening that I possessed supernatural strength at that moment.

Aiden gripped the rails on both sides of the wall, his veins bulging underneath the skin on his arms. He raised his head, looking over Hattie. "Run," he bit out, the skewed sunglasses allowing me to see one fully ambered eye. He hunched over, burying his face into my shoulder, giving me a clear view of the three darts protruding from his back and the grinning asshole at the top of the stairs.

"Hattie, run!" I screamed, trying to keep Aiden from crushing the both of us. She wriggled her way out from between me and Aiden and half scooted, half crawled down the rest of the staircase. I kept my eyes trained on the asshat who'd shot Aiden with what I was assuming was animal tranquilizers, until I heard her feet hit the carpeted floor below.

I slowly began my own descent down the stairs, but between walking backwards, and carrying Aiden's dead weight, I wasn't going nearly fast enough. Aiden's arm suddenly shot up, grabbing my shoulder. "Don't worry about me," he bit out in a raspy voice that didn't sound anything near human.

I was just about to tell him to shut the fuck up when I heard the sound of more darts being fired from my office, followed by Hattie's squeal and a hard thud. The man smirked at the look of desperation and defeat in my eyes. He pointed the tranq gun at me and leisurely stalked down the stairs, bringing his muted, but undeniable scent of wolf with him.

Realization dawned on me then. He snickered. "Figured out who I am, huh?"

The pulsing in my chest pounded harder, and I let my eyes turn. Baring my fangs at the rogue wolf, I hissed, "Fuck you."

I picked up my pace; I was almost to the bottom of the stairs. I knew I didn't stand much of a chance against him and whoever else was down in the office, but if I could just set Aiden down, I'd have a better shot at defending us than in my compromised state. Maybe someone more experienced at being a vampire could swing it, but fighting people while lugging a werewolf backwards down steps, just wasn't my forte.

When my feet hit the floor, I didn't have time to even sigh in relief before a figure stepped into my view, pointing another gun at me. Shock jolted through me, almost causing my grip on Aiden to weaken. "George?"

His innocent, youthful face twisted in a snarl. "Hello, *Riley*." Then he fired darts into my side.

I slumped down, Aiden's added weight making it impossible to try and fight the drugs. Whatever they were using was potent stuff. The effect was nearly immediate. My legs crumpled, making Aiden and I go down . . . hard. We landed, him on top of me, trapping me on the floor. It didn't matter, though. There was no way I could run away; I couldn't even feel my legs anymore.

I've never asked Lucian how far away he could pick up thoughts, and I knew it was a long shot, but I put the last bit of strength I had into shouting at him with my mind. I screamed and pleaded for him to hear me at that moment.

As the edges of my vision became increasingly blurry, the vampire gradually died down from my eyes. When George appeared, leaning over me with a sneer, I wondered what the hell I'd done to piss him off this badly.

Oh, yeah.

He'd almost died because of me. Was that it? Was this revenge for what happened?

I closed my eyes. I was so sleepy. One last fleeting thought crossed my mind before the darkness engulfed me: George had finally called me Riley.

CHAPTER 18

Weird smells were the first thing to assault my senses as I sluggishly woke up. Dampness, dirt, and something I suspiciously thought could be the smell of old death were among them. The next thing I could discern were the voices. I kept my eyes closed and my breathing steady as I tried to listen in.

"How long until they wake up?" George asked someone nervously.

"Don't tell me you're getting cold feet now?" a deep voice rumbled. I thought I recognized it as the rogue, but the timber was off. It was deeper and more guttural than it had been at the apartment.

"No," he protested, a little too quickly.

That only solicited a raucous laugh from the rogue. "Relax. Those handcuffs they're in will hold them, even if they do wake up while we're gone."

George gulped, making me fight back an evil grin. His betrayal was a fresh sting, and I hoped he pissed himself out of the fear that we'd wake up and take him out.

Soft footsteps echoed off the walls. "Ah, it must be time. She's on her way down here."

"How do you know?" I heard fabric shifting. "She didn't text me."

"I forget how pathetic you humans are," the rogue snarled. "I can hear her coming down the stairs."

"Really? That's so awesome."

This was just lovely. Here I was drugged and apparently—I still couldn't feel my body to check—handcuffed in a damp basement, while George was fangirling over the rogue.

The steps gradually became louder, until they abruptly stopped near me. "Come on, wolf. Malus says it's showtime." I'd know that voice anywhere.

"It's about fucking time." The rogue brushed past me. "Do you know how hard it is to fight the wolf when the moon is out?"

What the hell did they put in those darts? It was lunchtime when they surprised us at my apartment, and now it was already nighttime? The sun set around nine this time of year, so it had to be even later than that.

Dread filled me when I thought of Aiden. He was barely hanging on to control earlier. All he'd wanted was to get to pack land, so he could let his wolf out. Now he was trapped here with me, unconscious, and who knew what state he'd be in when he woke up. At least I assumed he was here with me. I tuned the voices out and concentrated on the other sounds in the room.

Counting six breathing forms, relief swept over me. Hattie and Aiden both had been dumped in the same room as me.

"I don't have time for this bullshit," Jessica sneered. "The tour group's gonna start any minute, and he wants you up there ready and waiting for them to pass by."

"Fine." The response came out more growl than anything, making it obvious he was fighting his own urges from the blood moon.

When their steps retreated far enough away, I risked opening an eye to peek at my surroundings. Vertigo hit when I realized I was laying down. Pushing past the nausea, I searched for my friends.

I saw Hattie first. She was leaning against a stone wall to my right, hands behind her back, and braced up on her side with a large wooden box. Aiden was to my left facing me, laying on some type of old metal gurney. He was stripped down to his boxer briefs, a chain wrapped around his torso, arms, and legs. Aiden's hands were also behind his back, and I could see another set of handcuffs clasped around his bare ankles.

George was standing with his back to me in a doorway, so I silently sat up. Flexing my fingers, I was thankful I was finally starting to feel my body again, and confirmed my wrists were shackled as well. My dry throat burned with hunger, and I blinked rapidly, trying to stave off the last remnants of bleariness, focusing on Aiden's ankles. The handcuffs looked suspiciously like the ones Everette and Gavin had the night before.

Fury swept through me, igniting the humming deep within me. Was this a confirmation of the BloodGuard's alliance with Malus, or was it just happenstance? Everette had said anyone who could afford them, could get them, but Sebastian had also warned us about Malus working with someone on the Low Council.

The pulsing in my chest began to die down, and I grasped for it, desperately trying to keep the power lit. If I could fuel it, maybe I could use my witch fire to get us out of here. I concentrated on it, but no matter how hard I tried, couldn't manage more than a steady thrum. I was simply too weak from the drugs still circulating in my system. Leaning my head back in defeat, I was at least grateful that I'd succeeded in keeping it alive. That was a start anyway.

This really needed to stop happening. Being kidnapped two times in a matter of months was a little ridiculous.

Hattie's breathing changed. I kept my eyes trained on her, waiting for her to stir. It wasn't long before she shifted, moaning at the stiffness I knew firsthand she was experiencing. "What the fuck, Riley?" she mumbled when she finally came to and glanced around the room.

"I'm so sorry, Hattie." I tried to scoot closer to her, but something was stopping me. I looked down to see one of my ankles cuffed to a metal loop protruding from the tile floor.

"I told you I had a bad feeling." She licked her lips. "Why don't you ever listen to me?"

"Really?" I snorted. "We're drugged, kidnapped, and wake up in some creepy basement, and that's what you're going with?" I raised an eyebrow. "That I should have listened to you?"

"That's enough." George stormed back in the room, holding up the dart gun. He pointed it back and forth between the two of us. "I'm telling you right now, if any of you tries anything, I'll shoot you faster than you can blink."

"Why?" I asked. "Why would you do this?"

"You're seriously asking me that?" he asked disbelievingly. "I figured you of all people would understand." When I just stared at him blankly, he huffed and elaborated, "Once I knew vampires and werewolves existed, I had to be one."

I groaned, rolling my eyes. "Could you be anymore cliché?"

"Could *you* be anymore naive?"

My teeth punched down, and I narrowed my eyes.

"Yeah, that's what I thought," he said smugly. "Anyway, when they came snooping around last month, I made a deal. I help them get to you, and in return, they change me into a vampire."

"Do you really believe that?" I bit out between tight lips. Now that my teeth were out on display, I was too weak to force them back into hiding. I knew Hattie was about to find out about me anyway, but I wasn't ready for her to see me like this.

"Of course. They just couldn't turn me yet because I needed to help them get to you first." He sounded confident, but I could see the doubt on his face. "They said you'd be able to tell if I was a vampire, and it would ruin the whole thing."

"You've got to be fucking kidding me. This is all because of vampires?" Hattie scooted up straighter, glaring at me. "Is that what your secret case was about? Fucking vampires? And now they're coming after you again?"

I didn't even know where to begin. I started and stopped several times, not being able to find the right words. How do you explain all the shit I've been through over the last few months to someone who wasn't already involved in this world?

Whatever she saw on my face, she didn't like. Hattie huffed, "Riley, why didn't you tell me about all this?"

"Oh, it gets even better." He stalked over to me, grabbed my head and pulled my lips back. I tried to stop him, but I was so weak. I needed blood. And I was certain that even if they did have blood bags lying around somewhere, there was no way in hell George was going to give me one. Or three. Or four. Who knew how much it would take to satiate my hunger and return my strength.

Hattie gasped when she saw the two elongated teeth, confirming that George wasn't batshit crazy and vampires really existed. He smirked and tossed me to the side. Not being able to brace myself, I hit the floor with a thunk, sending sharp pains radiating through my arm.

George's phone vibrated in his pocket. He pulled it out and aimed the gun at me again. "I have to take this. You'd better not try anything."

I grunted. "I can't, even if I wanted to."

"Good." He put the phone up to his ear. "Yeah?"

When he hurried out of the room to take his call, Aiden's eyes shot open, and he rattled the chains. Hattie gasped again when she saw the fury in his amber eyes.

"Riley, we don't have much time," he grunted in the same deep, guttural voice as the rogue had before he left with Jessica. "These chains are silver. But if I could just get them off . . .," he trailed off.

"Don't hurt yourself, Aiden." Everywhere the silver touched, there were angry red stripes. I knew he had to be in tremendous pain.

"I can't believe this," Hattie murmured, shaking her head.

"Hattie, I'm so sorry," I pleaded. "Please don't look at me any differently, or be mad at me."

She raised up on her knees. "I promise I won't be mad at you, if you won't be mad at me," She started muttering in a language I'd never heard before. I struggled back up to a sitting position, watching her with curiosity. The handcuffs glowed dimly, then fell off her wrists once she finished her incantation.

My eyes widened. "You're a witch!" I hissed. How was it possible that all along, everyone in my life were supernaturals, and I had no fucking clue?

She pointed a finger at me. "You don't have any room to judge." Sitting back, she brought her knees up to her chest and did the spell again to the cuffs I hadn't noticed on her ankles.

She crawled over to me. "Where is he?"

"At the end of the hallway, still on his phone." Wherever we were must've been massive. I could tell he'd walked a good distance away. And when Jessica came down there to get the rogue, it had taken her a while to reach us.

"We have to make this quick." Hattie repeated the spell twice, once for my wrists and the other for my ankle. I rubbed my wrists, relieved to have them off. "Okay, time to go all vampy and take that guy down."

"I can't."

"What do you mean you can't?" she angrily whispered at me.

"I mean, I've been drugged and haven't had blood for over twelve hours on the night of a blood moon." Being this close, I could smell the blood running underneath her skin. I fought the urge to bite into my best friend to get the sustenance my body so desperately needed. "Why don't you go all witchy on George and take him out with a spell, or a fireball, or whatever it is your family's line can do."

215

Her lips pursed. Apparently, I'd hit a nerve. "My family's special talent is seeing glimpses of the future. Which," she held up a hand, stopping me from asking any questions, "isn't very strong with me. And even if it was, it wouldn't help us in this situation." She tried, and failed to help me stand. "And I was never very interested in being a witch, so I only know basic spells and incantations."

"So, basically you're a shitty witch?"

Hattie tried not to crack a smile. "Yeah. And you're a useless vampire."

"I'm not useless," I protested. "I'm just thirsty."

"So, how are a shitty witch and a thirsty vampire going to get out of here?"

"Drink from me, Riley," Aiden spoke up. "Take what you need, then get me out of these chains."

"Aiden, I don't think that's a good idea." I knew he was in pain, but I was afraid he'd lose control if the silver was removed. And as appealing as the prospect was to have blood, I didn't even want to entertain his offer.

He growled, making Hattie freeze beside me. "I know you don't want to take a vein, but if you want you and Hattie to survive this, you're going to have to. You can't fight them off in your condition." Why did he have to make sense right now? "You can't take blood from Hattie. You're too weak, and you've never taken a vein before, so you might not stop in time."

Before I even realized what I was doing, I was crawling toward Aiden. "What if I can't stop with you?"

"You will. Little known fact about werewolf blood . . . it's very potent. You won't need as much of mine as you would a human." George ended his call, giving way to panic in Avery's eyes. "Hurry." He growled. "Drink. Get your strength, then set me free. I can control it, I promise."

My eyes changed as I reached Aiden, looking him over, trying to find the best place to bite. Since chains covered most of his body, the only logical place was his throat. But that seemed a little too intimate. And I couldn't believe I was going to do this, anyway. Taking a vein, other than Lucian's, was something I said I never wanted to do. But he was right. If we were going to get out of here, I needed to be at full strength. And this was the only way to do that.

George started walking down the hallway, back toward our room. Aiden bared his neck. "Just do it, Riley."

I pulled myself up to my knees and glanced down at Aiden, giving him one more chance to tell me to stop. His only response was a growl, so I leaned down to his throat, breathing in the musky, woodsy scent of Aiden. Beneath his usual fragrance was the aroma of blood. My mouth watered. It smelled so good, and I wondered why I'd never noticed his blood like that before.

I positioned my teeth over the vein I knew would give me what I needed. Aiden shuddered, and I hesitated. His chest rumbled in a strange purry growl, giving me a final warning to hurry the hell up. I pushed away any reluctance I had left and bit down, my teeth easily piercing his skin.

The first rush of warm blood hit my tongue, bringing an unsolicited moan from me. It wasn't like anything I'd ever tasted before. Lucian's fresh blood was a stark difference from blood bags, but I still felt more nourished after drinking them than I did Lucian's. Aiden's blood was like a balmy shot of pure adrenaline. With each gulp I could feel the strength returning to my body. If drinking from a human vein was anything like this, I could understand the appeal.

"How the hell did you get over there?" George screeched. I reluctantly withdrew my teeth, turning just in time to see Hattie smack him over the head with a board. His eyes rolled in the back of his head, and he fell to the floor.

"Just because I'm a shitty witch, doesn't mean I still can't take someone down." Hattie beamed, dropping her wooden weapon on top of him, for good measure.

"Oh yeah? Let's how you do against me," Jessica said from the doorway. She must have snuck down here while I was feeding from Aiden. I'd been so caught up in the blood rush, I didn't hear or sense her.

Jessica stepped toward Hattie, and I lunged to get in front of my friend. Bloody fangs bared, I snarled. "Stay away from her."

"This is why I just wanted to kill you and get it over with. You're too much trouble." She entered the room, giving us a wide berth. "But Malus insisted on keeping you alive. He still thinks you can be persuaded to join us."

I cocked my head to the side. "Attacking people close to me isn't a very good way of winning me over."

"Oh, that was all me. He wanted werewolf attacks, so I picked the targets."

So, it was her fault Jeremy was a shifter now and Trevor was dead. I reached my arm back, ushering Hattie to move closer to Aiden. Between his powerful blood and Jessica's admission, my entire body was now buzzing with witch energy. If I let my fire loose, I had no idea how it would manifest, and I didn't want her to accidentally get hurt.

"And why are we here?" I gestured to the room. "What's Malus planning?"

"We needed someplace where there would be a lot of people with cameras, but no police. There was only one obvious choice in Louisville."

"But why here? Why come back to Louisville?"

"Don't you get it? The original plan is still the same. We want to come out of hiding. But this time, we've got a wolf to do it with us." She edged closer to me. "And coming back here to do it was more for revenge than anything else."

She dove at me without warning, but I saw her coming. I pivoted at the last second, grabbed her by the shoulders, and swung her around, throwing her into the wall. Wiping a drop of blood from her mouth, she slowly rose back up. "You'll pay for that."

She leapt through the air, pouncing on top of me, sending both of us barreling to the ground. No sooner had I landed, I sprung up to a crouching position. She mimicked my actions, curling her lips back with a hiss.

Hattie's panicked voice began chanting the same incantation she'd used to free both of us, so I could only assume she was doing the same with Aiden's two sets of spelled cuffs. Jessica jerked her head in their direction, and I thrust forward, tackling her before she could realize what Hattie was doing. We rolled for several feet before she was able to kick me away from her.

The inner heat spread rapidly down my arms as I jumped up in a defensive position. I let the warmth build, just shy of flowing into my hands while she took the same stance I did. We circled each other, both sizing up the other one, waiting for the perfect opportunity to attack.

219

Her leg tensed, alerting me she about to spring forward, and I released the fire into my palms. It was like a dam bursting, and it felt so fucking good. My hands lit up in blue dancing flames, casting the entire room in a cerulean glow.

Jessica's eyes grew about two sizes larger before she darted for the door. But there was no way I was going to let her get away. I didn't have time to think, my body just reacted. The flame on my hand morphed into a round shape, I cocked my arm back and released it, just as I had playing baseball as a kid in gym class.

The fire ball hit her square in the back just as she crossed the doorway. With an ear-splitting screech, she went down. I rushed over, another ball ready to go in my palm in case the first one wasn't enough, but at the sight of her seared back, I internally cringed. Jessica's shirt was in singed tatters, displaying the blackened, smoking skin beneath.

Whimpering, she tried to crawl away. "I don't think so." I let the flames recede, until the humming in my chest was the only evidence left of my witch fire, grabbed her by the legs, and dragged her back into the room.

"You have a lot of explaining to do," Hattie said, as she started unraveling the chains from Aiden's torso.

"I know." I sighed, dropping Jessica's legs. "But so do you."

"Trust me, I know." She glanced up at me. "As soon as we get out of here, we're going to need an entire afternoon and a lot of alcohol."

I crossed my arms. "Agreed."

With a menacing growl, Aiden threw off the last of the chains. He slowly rose to all fours, the muscles rippling underneath his skin.

Hattie and I exchanged a look. "Aiden, are you going to be okay?"

Panting heavily, he raised his head, pinning me with glowing amber eyes. "I'll be fine."

I wasn't convinced, but I let it go. I needed to take care of Jessica first, then I'd worry about the werewolf in the room.

Hattie reached down, picking up the discarded cuffs and walked over to me and Jessica. "Let's see how they like these."

We needed to get out of there fast. Whatever Malus had planned wasn't going to be good. A place with a lot of cameras, no police, and a werewolf ready to shift under a full moon was not a combination that would end well. Especially since the rogue was already getting into position, waiting for a group of humans to pass by his location.

Jessica and George would only slow us down during our rush to get out of there, so we decided to leave them in the room for now. Chained and as injured as Jessica was, there was no way they would be able to get free and warn Malus. Once we escaped and called for backup, we'd go back down and get them.

"You won't be able to stop him," Jessica feebly sniveled as Hattie and I worked together, chaining Jessica up to the same metal loop that I'd been attached to.

"We'll see about that." I clasped the cuffs on her wrists tighter than necessary, getting instant gratification when she moaned in discomfort. I moved on to the still unconscious George as Hattie draped the silver chains over Jessica for added assurance.

By the time we finished, Aiden was standing and seemingly in control. But it didn't escape my notice that both his top and bottom canines were now longer than the rest of his teeth. And noticeably sharper.

"Are you good?" he rumbled.

My eyes drifted to the healing puncture marks on his neck. I was more than good. I'd never felt this amazing in my life. But did I want more of his blood? Hell yes. "I don't need anymore." I was already going to have a hard enough time drinking bags after that one feeding from him, there was no way I'd be able to go back to them if I drank from Aiden again. "Thank you, Aiden."

"Do you guys have any idea where we are?" Hattie scrutinized the room we were standing in.

Tile covered the floor and large sections of the stone walls. Broken pieces laid scattered all across the floor, along with several more metal loops like the one I'd been chained to, stacks of damp papers, rotting wooden boxes, and what looked like antique medical equipment.

I shook my head. "I have no idea." But it didn't matter. We just needed to get out of there before Malus or the rogue decided to show up.

As if reading my thoughts, Aiden stalked over to the door. "Let's just get the fuck out of here."

I couldn't have agreed more, but first we were going to need something from George. I hurried back over to his crumpled form and searched his pockets. Pulling out his cell phone, I immediately dialed Lucian's number, and without a backward glance, followed Aiden out.

CHAPTER 19

We followed Jessica's scent, easily finding a narrow concrete stairwell at the end of the hallway. Her trail went up farther, but we decided to exit after climbing only one flight, and were on, what we assumed, was the ground floor. The goal was to escape, not find Malus. At least, not yet.

Aiden cracked the heavy door as quietly as possible and the three of us slipped through the slim opening. In the distance, I could hear countless people talking in nervous and excited tones. I inhaled sharply, taking in more of the same scents as the basement, the only main addition was the stench of human sweat.

It was obvious wherever we were didn't have air conditioning, and that wasn't a good mix for a humid Kentucky summer night and what sounded like at least a hundred perspiring humans. I scrunched my nose and glanced around, but nothing noticeably gave away our location.

"It's the same smells on this floor, but there's a lot of humans somewhere in here," I whispered to Lucian on the phone. "And there's no air conditioning. Wait." I breathed in again. "I can smell the night air."

"It's this way." Aiden bounded in the opposite direction of where the people were congregated. Silently cursing, I trailed after him.

"Wait for me!" Hattie cried out, bringing up the rear.

"What's going on?" Lucian demanded.

When he'd answered my call, he'd been a frantic mess, demanding to know where I was and profusely apologizing for letting this happen to me again. I tried to tell him it wasn't his fault, but he persisted until I finally just gave up. I needed to figure out where we were, so I could relay it to him for backup, not waste my time arguing with him about who was to blame for my second kidnapping by Malus.

"Aiden's leading us out of the building." As we ran down this new hallway, I kept my eye out for any identifying markers, but there were none. It was just room after room of what looked like offices that hadn't been used since before I was born. We turned a corner, and relief swept through me. "He found an exit door."

"Thank goodness." I heard car doors slamming shut and an engine hum to life through the phone. "We're in the vehicle, ready to leave as soon as you can find out where you are."

We bound through the door, into the open night, and only made it about fifty feet before Aiden and I both stopped in our tracks and looked to the sky. The eclipse had already begun, the moon was almost completely hidden. It wouldn't be long before it appeared as a reddish globe in the night sky.

I closed my eyes, basking in what was left of the moonlight. I wasn't sure if it was Aiden's wolf blood, the pull of the blood moon, the witch power humming in my body, or a combination of all three, but at that moment I felt invincible. There was no holding back my vampire, so I didn't even try. And if felt good to let it out. A little too good.

A chilling snarl rippled through the night, letting me know that Aiden was just as affected by the moon above us as I was. "Riley, is Aiden alright?" Lucian must've heard him through the phone.

Looking him over, I could see he was visibly struggling to contain the beast. His face was contorted in anguished restraint, and his skin rippled with the wolf trying to break free. Aiden nodded, letting me know he had it under control . . . at least for now. "Yeah, but I don't know for how long."

Poor Hattie was clearly nervous, and I couldn't blame her. Even though she was a witch, she was admittedly not a very good one, and here she was stuck with a vampire in full-on vamp mode and a werewolf ready to shed his skin and run amuck under a full moon. I could only imagine what was going through her mind.

I started to offer her some words of comfort when a flashlight shining behind and above her distracted me. Studying our surroundings for the first time since we'd fled the building, a sense of dread filled me. The light was coming from the second floor, where people were roaming the hallways and long-abandoned patient rooms searching for signs of ghosts and spirits.

Taking a few steps back, I inspected the building in its entirety, just to make sure what I suspected was true. As much as I didn't want to admit it, there was no mistaking the uniquely shaped building looming before me. Of all the places they could've taken us, of course it had to be this one. "Lucian, I know where we are." I sighed in resignation. "Waverly Hills Sanatorium."

∞ ∞ ∞

It had been about ten minutes since I hung up with Lucian. And if traffic cooperated, he and the BloodGuards would be there in another twenty. He didn't go into much detail over the phone, but he did say that Everette and Gavin had returned earlier in the day, saying they wanted to get back as soon as possible because they had a feeling something was going down tonight. What Lucian didn't say aloud, but I knew he was thinking, was if they wanted to be here to help us against Malus, or to make sure we didn't stop him.

In the meantime, the three of us retreated to the tree line waiting for them to arrive. We didn't want anyone to see us wandering around the grounds and get suspicious. Plus, Aiden and I needed the small reprieve the trees gave us from the direct moon light. We could still feel the pull from the moon, like a beacon in the sky, but not being out in the open dampened the effect somewhat.

Standing there, glowering up at Waverly, I had to give it to Malus for his creativity. He wanted to make sure there would be plenty of cameras to catch supernaturals in action, but no police interference to take them down. That wouldn't be possible at any major events around Louisville or heavily populated areas like bars and clubs. Those places would be swarming with security and cops.

But at Waverly? There may have been a security guard or two, but that was about it. And every single person in that place had their cameras and phones already out recording and taking pictures. The footage would be one click away from being an internet sensation. It was brilliant—if that's what you wanted. I definitely didn't want to be outed, and I knew most of the supernaturals around here didn't, either. If humans knew about us, there was no telling what would happen. We could be hunted, caged like animals, experimented on, and the list went on and on.

"So, what's the plan exactly?" Hattie was a frightened, nervous wreck, constantly fidgeting the entire time we'd been out there. I wanted to tell her to calm the fuck down, because I could smell her fear—which was something I didn't even know I could do before now—and it had an alluring spice to it that made my throat itch with want, but I knew that would only freak her out even more. And from the way Aiden was pacing and throwing daggers in her direction, I could tell her fear was just as appealing to his beast as it was to my vampire.

"We wait out here in the trees until Lucian gets here. Then we sneak in and take care of Malus once and for all."

She put a hand on her hip. "And what if he starts attacking people before they get here?"

A deep reverberation emitted from the depths of Aiden's chest. "Then we run in there and take those bastards out."

"Look, I don't want anyone to get hurt, but I also don't want to be filmed like this." I gestured at my face. The preternatural agility I'd be showing off, combined with my vampire eyes and pointy teeth would be a dead giveaway to what I was. If any one of them uploaded the footage, it wouldn't take much to recognize me, and then who knows who or what would be coming after me.

Aiden snarled. "I don't care. Let them film. It's not like they won't already have enough proof from whatever they capture of Malus and the rogue before we can take them down."

Yeah, easy for him to say. They wouldn't be capturing his face to distribute to the masses, only his beast form. He'd be able to go on about his business with no one the wiser.

But for the sake of not pissing him off, and further adding fuel to his wolf's fire, I kept my mouth shut and didn't point that out to him. Instead, I turned to Hattie, "Regardless of how we handle either situation, I think you should stay out here."

"I'm not staying out here while you all put yourselves in danger."

"Hattie, you said yourself that you don't know many spells, and since you don't have super strength or any other ability like that, you're more than likely the one who's going to get hurt." Being the only one told to stay behind just last night, I understood all too well how she felt. But this was different. Besides having the gift of being able to perform spells, witches were more human than any of the other supernatural species. They were mortal and healed at a human's pace. Vampires could live for centuries and both vamps and werewolves healed at a rapid rate, making them harder to kill.

"Just because I don't know many spells, doesn't mean I don't know *any*."

Screams abruptly erupted from inside Waverly Hills preventing any type of rebuttal I had for her. I looked at George's phone, then around the grounds in search of our backup. They should be there any minute. If we could just hold out a little bit longer, we would have three experienced vampires to go in with us.

A daunting howl echoed through the sanatorium, followed by more terrified shrieks. Aiden fell to the ground, tremors wracking his body. Hattie and I both backed away from him, wide-eyed. I'd seen them in their wolf form before, but I'd never seen any of them actually go through the change. His skin ripped, bones contorted, his face elongated giving way to a snout, black hair sprouted over his entire body, and his ears lengthened to points.

The entire process only took a matter of seconds, and where Aiden had fallen, now crouched a wolf-like beast. He slowly rose to stand on two awkwardly bent hind legs and shook off the last remnants of the change. Aiden sniffed the air, then focused his amber gaze directly on me. I knew they retained some semblance of their human mind when they shifted, but I had no idea if that held true during the blood moon. "Aiden?" I whispered.

His lips pulled back from his snout, and he tilted his head up and down once. I released the breath I hadn't realized I'd been holding, and the tension left my body. Aiden's ears twitched, and before I could even try to stop him, he fell on all fours and bounded toward the old hospital.

"Shit." I took a few steps, scanning the area again for any signs of Lucian or the BloodGuard.

Hattie took off after Aiden, yelling over her shoulder, "Sorry, but I can't sit back and not help."

229

Cursing again, I launched after them. The last thing I wanted was to be the face of the newly outed vampires, but I also would never forgive myself if I could've prevented a single death and didn't, so I wouldn't have to deal with that.

It didn't take long to catch up to Hattie, but I kept going, pushing past her and into the building. I followed Aiden's scent, which led me closer and closer to the screams. Racing up a much larger staircase than the one we'd used to escape from the basement, I ran into several people hysterically fleeing down them, trying to get away from whatever was going on above us.

I tried to keep my head down, but a few of them spotted my eyes and began shouting that I was one of them, which only caused more of a frenzy to ensue. I brushed it off and kept going. It didn't matter if they were afraid of me, I'd still fight to save them regardless.

When I reached the fourth floor, the only humans left—who were either brave or stupid, depending on how you looked at it—were the ones with their phones held out, recording the scene before me. Aiden and the rogue were locked in a snarling battle of teeth and claws. I slowly advanced, trying to figure out how I could help Aiden. There was no way I could use my witch fire with all these innocent people here. I had no control over it yet, and I was trying to help them, not make things worse by setting them or the building on fire.

I knew Aiden was the smaller one, the fur was the same color as the wolf I'd seen outside. The other larger wolf was lighter brown with red tints mixed in the hair. The rogue clearly had the size advantage and was trying to use that against Aiden. But Aiden was more agile and faster than his opponent. The hallway we were in was large by human standards, but for two fighting werewolves not so much. There was only so much dodging Aiden was going to be able to do before he tired and slipped up.

As I neared the back of the spectators, my skin erupted in the tell-tale tingling warning, and I tensed, knowing exactly who it was for. It had the same chilling sensation I'd felt at the gas station in PRP when Malus had been near. The air shifted behind me, and I knew he was there.

"Hello, Riley," he breathed in my ear.

"Malus," I acknowledged, not turning around. I had to think fast. I didn't have any weapons, and I knew I was no match for him even if I did.

"I see you escaped." He came up beside me. "Tell me, what did you do with Jessica?"

"Why don't you go and see for yourself?"

"Ha!" he barked out, startling a few of the humans closest to us.

"It's him. The vampire," one of them whispered.

"I think she's one, too," another said as they raised their phone to record me and Malus. This was just great.

"I knew you would be a formidable vampire." Malus blocked them out of my view, moving to stand in front of me. "That's why I wanted you."

Putting my big girl panties on, I glared up into his crystal-blue eyes. "Fuck you." He smiled, and I hated to admit how handsome he was. Malus somehow had delicate, but masculine facial features, long white hair that girls nowadays would pay a fortune to get, and a smooth seductive voice.

"That could be arranged as well." At the sight of disgust on my face, he tsked me. "Don't be so hasty to judge. We are, after all, the same."

"I'm nothing like you."

"You'd be surprised what you'll be like after a few centuries."

I didn't have a retort for that one. Lucian was pushing two hundred, and he'd managed to retain his humanness, but I'd seen others, like those vampires from House Moretti that were barely even legal and didn't have an ounce of humanity left in them. All I could do was hope that I'd be more like Lucian and retain my human morals through the years.

"I have to say, you were a beautiful human, but now that you're vampire, you are truly exquisite." He began circling me. "You know there's still time. You can still join my cause."

"Like I said before, fuck you."

"Very well." Malus took a step back, his lips set in a firm line. "But we'll see whose side you're on after tonight." Chills spread down my spine from the sadistic smile that spread across his face.

One second he was staring down at me like the crazed maniac he was, the next he was biting into one of our human onlookers. Panicked, I lunged for him, trying to pry him off of the human, but he swatted me away as easily as I could a fly.

My back slammed into the wall, knocking the breath out of me. I shook it off and charged after him again, this time leaping onto his back. Wrapping my legs around his torso, I grabbed his head, jerking it backward. The fresh human blood assaulted my senses, and I fought hard to stay focused and not gorge on it myself.

He dropped the human, only to dive for the one next to him. Malus only had enough time to plunge his teeth in the guy's neck and get a gulp or two before I was able to pull his head away again. Letting out a frustrated growl, he jumped backward, crashing me into the wall again. I held on firmly, but when he repeated the action twice more, my hold slipped, and I slid off of his back.

Malus twisted and grabbed me by the throat, raising me up against the wall, my feet dangling in the air. I clutched his hand, trying to pry his fingers loose. The heat spread down my arms, but I held it back. I couldn't risk hurting anyone besides Malus. "It's too late now. You might as well stop trying to fight the inevitable."

"Never," I managed to rasp.

"Or is it that you're jealous?" He licked his blood-covered lips "Would you rather it was you I was feasting on instead of those useless humans?" Malus used his other hand to rip the neck of my t-shirt, exposing my shoulder. When he started to lean toward my flesh, I kicked him right between the legs with everything I had.

"Fuck!" he swore, releasing his hold on me. I dropped to the floor and rolled away from him as fast as I could.

"Riley!" Lucian yelled from the top of the stairs.

Tears of joy sprang to my eyes at the sight of him. I started to run toward him, but something snapped me backward, landing me against a hard chest. A strong arm snaked around my waist, and I felt the coldness of a knife against my throat. "That wasn't very nice," Malus hissed.

Lucian sprinted for us, but stopped about fifteen feet away, when Malus pressed the knife harder against my skin. "That will be far enough, Lucian. Or I'll slit her throat."

Lucian bared his fangs. "You draw one drop of blood from her, and I'll tear you limb from limb."

Malus chuckled. "You can try. You may even succeed, although I highly doubt that. But either way, she'll be dead." He backed us up, passing a doorway to an old patient room. A teenage girl was leaning against it, holding her arm and crying. It looked suspiciously like a claw mark wound, and I wondered how many people the rogue had attacked before Aiden showed up, distracting him from his mission. "I can, however, offer another solution."

Lucian stepped in time with us, careful to maintain the same distance. "I'm listening."

I narrowed my eyes at him, but he ignored me. He wasn't seriously going to consider anything Malus was going to offer, right? The guy was insane. I glanced behind Lucian to see what Everette and Gavin were doing, but they weren't anywhere to be seen. I knew they were with Lucian when he left, so if they weren't with him now to fight Malus, there could only be one reason for that . . . they were working with him.

"Join my cause. As you can see, it's already too late to stop me."

Lucian fleetingly skimmed over the hallway, seeing firsthand how many people were witnessing this little display. "And what would that entail?"

A howl of pain sounded behind us, making me cringe. I had no idea if it came from Aiden or the rogue. "For the long term? We'll make the humans submit to us, as it should be."

"And for the short term?"

Tingles spread on my skin. There was another vampire here.

"For now, you can prove your allegiance by killing most of these wretched humans. We only need a few alive, so they can share what they've seen tonight."

Lucian rubbed his jaw. "I think I'll take another option."

"There is no other option!" Malus roared.

"I assure you there is." Lucian smirked. "Let me enlighten you."

A brute force slammed into us, knocking both of us down. Malus's grip released, and the knife clattered to the floor. I hastily snatched it up, springing to my feet, ready to attack Malus if he came after me again.

"Riley." Lucian grabbed my face, pulling my gaze from the sight of Gavin punching Malus in the face, and gently moved my head around, checking for wounds.

"I'm fine," I assured him. Actually, my entire body hurt, but now wasn't the time to divulge that to him. He pulled me to him and kissed me. It was one of those searing, toe-curling, I'm madly in love with you, kisses.

Hattie came running up beside us, panting for breath. "Do you know how hard that is to run all the way up here from that tree line when you haven't exercised since high school?" She sucked in a deep breath. "Seriously, why isn't there a working elevator in this bitch?"

Lucian broke away from me. "I'll be back. Stay here."

He produced his own knife and joined Gavin in the fight against Malus. Lucian slashed out, catching Malus in the arm. He cried out, giving Gavin the split-second opportunity to drive his own into Malus's chest. Shock registered on his face, but he swung out, connecting with Gavin's head.

Gavin went down, but Malus's reflexes weren't as fast now that he had a knife protruding from his body, so Lucian was able to drive his knife into Malus's back multiple times. Gavin pulled a dagger from his boot, slicing through Malus's Achilles tendon on the back of both his ankles.

Blood gushed from the wounds, already pooling at Malus's feet, and he dropped to his knees. Lucian grabbed Malus by his hair, pulling his head back. "This is for kidnapping the woman I love not once, but twice." Lucian stabbed him in the chest, close to the knife still sticking out, and twisted it around, until blood poured from the wound. One he was satisfied Malus wasn't surviving after that injury, Lucian tossed him to the floor.

Lucian looked to me, eyes blazing and lips parted, revealing a peek at his fangs, and something deep down inside me wanted nothing more than to pounce on him where he stood. I wanted to roll around in the blood with Lucian, both of us gorging on each other and him pounding into me, until we were spent.

Heat flared in his eyes. "You wanted to know what the blood moon does to us? That's what." He tapped his head, letting me know he'd picked up loud and clear what I'd been thinking. "It brings our true nature to the forefront, with no inhibitions to deter it."

An ear-splitting howl behind us, garnered all of our attention. Everette was trying and failing to get a good swipe at the rogue with his knife. Aiden and the rogue were still locked in a deadly fight, and I could see multiple wounds on both wolves. Every time Everette got close to the rogue, they would shift, and he'd lose his chance.

Hattie cracked her knuckles. "I got this." She held up her hands and muttered a spell, focusing on the battling werewolves. As soon as she finished, the rogue yelped and fell backward. Everette and Aiden both took advantage and pounced on him at the same time. Aiden tore into him with his mouth, and I looked away.

"You're a witch?" Lucian looked between Hattie and me.

"Yeah, but I don't know many spells. Luckily for us, I memorized any of them I could use to torture my younger brother." She pointed to the wolves. "That one was a tripping spell."

"Seriously?" I raised an eyebrow. "There's a spell for something stupid like that?"

She snorted. "You'd be surprised what there's spells for. And that stupid spell just let us win."

"Touché."

Malus wheezed. "You know this is just the beginning." He coughed, and blood spurted out of his mouth. "My mission has been completed." Glaring at Gavin, he added, "You were supposed to be on my side."

Gavin placed his hands on his hips. "Not likely."

The vampire glow slowly left Malus's eyes. "Riley, it would have been better if you were mine." He coughed again, a steady stream of blood now trickling from the corner of his mouth. "I was going to keep you." Malus gasped for air. "Protect you." He closed his eyes, his next words barely louder than a whisper. "But now, he'll kill you."

I couldn't believe it. As many times as I'd wished for Malus to die, when he actually did, I wanted him to come back. Who would kill me? I thought once Malus was gone, my worries would be over.

Cheers erupted from all around us. We turned around, seeing the faces of a dozen or so humans who'd stayed hidden in the patient rooms, watching that entire scene unfold. And every one of them had a phone pointed toward us.

"What do we do?" I asked Lucian, as Everette and an injured Aiden in wolf form came up next to us.

"I'm afraid there's nothing we can do."

"I have a feeling things are about to get interesting," Everette said, flashing his flirtatious smile at a group of girls and winking at them.

I had a feeling things were going to get more than interesting. And I could only hope that it took a long time for anyone to recognize me on those videos.

EPILOGUE

A small group of us had gathered on *Silver Moon's* main dance floor to watch the debate on the news. Lucian had a large white screen hanging from the stage and a digital projector setup, streaming the live feed. It had only taken a day for the videos to become viral, but almost two weeks to verify their authenticity and garner the attention of the media and world-wide leaders.

So far, no one had come forward saying they recognized us and knew our identities, but I knew it was only a matter of time. Lucian was hands-on at the club and well-known by the patrons, both supernatural and human alike, so it was inevitable that he'd be outed eventually. I'd been on edge since that night, waiting for people to show up with torches and pitch forks, demanding to stake us in our coffins.

Once the fight was over, we didn't hesitate to clean up our mess and get the hell out of there before the police could show up. Alex pulled up with a blackout van, and between all of us, we loaded Malus, the rogue, Jessica, and George into the back.

Aiden also rode in the van, so he could keep an eye on Jessica. Plus, he wouldn't be able to shift back until the following morning, and he needed the extra space for his wolf body.

Everette and Gavin left shortly after that to transport all those involved, dead or alive, to the BloodGuard headquarters. Turns out, they actually were on our side. They said the assignment seemed shady from the start, but they accepted it anyway since the other two members of their unit would be fine for a few days by themselves where they were currently stationed.

When they had delivered the boys responsible for the vampire murders to House Moretti, they got a message requesting them to hold off on returning to Louisville until after the blood moon. When they asked why, the only response they received was that it would be in their best interest. Apparently, they didn't like following rules, despite the fact they enforced them for a living. I was really starting to warm up to both of them.

But that did mean that *someone* in the BloodGuard, and consequently the Low Council, had known what Malus was planning and didn't want Everette and Gavin to interfere. They verified that they never knew who made the assignments; they came from a dispatch-like center, so unless they started asking questions, they wouldn't have any idea who the culprit was. As soon as things settled down with the media, they were going to start digging for information because they said they couldn't sit back and watch while the BloodGuard became compromised.

So far, we'd seen mixed reactions to the knowledge that supernaturals existed and were living among humans. Some were ecstatic, many people were still skeptical about the validity of the footage, and others were borderline hostile. I'd been keeping an eye on the televised debates and major internet blogs, and I heard everything from death threats to marriage proposals when it came to us. To say the whole thing was surreal would be an understatement.

"Ah, here it is." Lucian turned the volume up. "Everyone, please be quiet," he called out from his seat next to me. He gripped my hand, squeezing tight, as we waited to hear the current consensus from some of the most influential people in the country.

As the debate about us raged on, everyone from celebrities to university professors had weighed in with their opinions. And while there had been some political leaders speaking publicly on the topic, for the most part, they'd been tight-lipped about their plans on whether or not to take any actions toward us. A small group of prominent people from society—three CEO's, one producer, two world-renown scientists, a couple of news anchors, and a handful of others—were currently gathering for a televised discussion about what they thought the next step should be concerning supernaturals in the United States.

We had no idea how this was going to go, and I could tell Lucian was nervous about what they were about to say. These people held a lot of influence over the average citizen, so depending on their stances, it could lead to more people being content with our shared existence, or a longer line of them waiting to drive stakes in our hearts.

And while not all people in power knew about us before our outing, there were many that did. They were people who could've vouched for us and reminded the public that we'd always been there sharing the world with them, the only difference now was that they knew about it. But to save face, they were acting like they had no idea we'd existed until those videos were released. I thought it was bullshit. But what could I do about it?

For now, the plan was for all of us to lay as low as possible and not draw any attention to ourselves. I did go ahead and re-open my office, but it was mainly to pre-existing customers and only a select few new ones that Aiden graciously pre-vetted for me. And for the time being, Lucian wasn't making any appearances in the club during business hours. So, all we really could do was sit back and wait to see what the new future had in store for us.

∞ ∞ ∞

AUTHOR'S NOTE

Thank you so much for reading *Blood Moon*! I hope you enjoyed the second installment of the Riley Hunter Series. If so and you would like to help support the series, I would appreciate it if you could leave an honest review on Amazon, Goodreads, and/or anywhere else. Reviews are a great way to support your favorite authors!

∞ ∞ ∞

The third full-length novel in the Riley Hunter Series, *Hunter's Moon*, will be available in the summer of 2019.

Want to know more about Ellie? Find out where she came from and which member of the BloodGuard stole her heart. Order Ellie's short novella, *Dark Betrayal-A Riley Hunter Prequel* today.

CONNECT WITH AMANDA LYNN

∞ ∞ ∞

Follow to stay updated on new releases:

Facebook
Twitter
Instagram
Website

Keep up to date on everything Amanda Lynn. Sign up for the mailing list.

BOOKS BY AMANDA LYNN

THE RILEY HUNTER SERIES:

Silver Moon

Blood Moon

Hunter's Moon-Release Summer 2019

RILEY HUNTER WORLD:

Dark Betrayal

THE BLOODGUARD SERIES:

Book 1 (Continuation of Ellie & Kade's story)-Late 2019

∞ ∞ ∞

CPSIA information can be obtained
at www.ICGtesting.com
Printed in the USA
BVHW031253190420
577913BV00001B/165